The Knife Thrower

'The prose is beautiful and meticulously crafted, yet always summoning what is just beyond the power of words . . . Millhauser is a master storyteller' *Time Out*

'Millhauser's forte is finding new ways of dramatising the American Dream as it turns, so often and so easily, into a kind of waking nightmare . . . Clever and intriguing'

Literary Review

'While these stories are arrestingly original, they also have an ageless mythic quality. Written with deadpan accuracy and fastidious detachment, they are unforgettable'

Harper's & Queen

'As sinister as it is fanciful . . . [*The Knife Thrower*] is Millhauser at his purest' *San Francisco Chronicle*

'Millhauser draws us effortlessly into the shimmering worlds of his fictions. His writing has a rare quality that is hard to resist' *Boston Globe*

'Curious and tantalising . . . Millhauser's own ingenuity is delicious . . . The strength and glitter of its imaginative grip lies in Millhauser's ability to weave detail into detail, the lovingly real and possible into the extravagantly impossible'
A. S. Byatt, *Washington Post*

'Splendid flashes of absurdity and satire. Millhauser has a rich, sly sense of humour . . . in his exploration of the complicated response we have to the products and projections of our own minds, Millhauser is without equal among contemporary writers' *New York Times Book Review*

Steven Millhauser was born in New York City and grew up in Connecticut. His stories have appeared in various publications including the *New Yorker* and *Esquire*. His most recent novel, *Martin Dressler*, was the winner of the 1997 Pulitzer Prize for Fiction and was also shortlisted for the US National Book Award. Steven Millhauser teaches at Skidmore College and lives with his wife and two children in Saratoga Springs, New York.

BY THE SAME AUTHOR

Martin Dressler: The Tale of an American Dreamer
The Barnum Museum
From the Realm of Morpheus
In the Penny Arcade
Little Kingdoms
Portrait of a Romantic
Edwin Mullhouse: The Life and Death of an
American Writer

The Knife Thrower
and Other Stories

STEVEN MILLHAUSER

PHŒNIX

A PHOENIX PAPERBACK

First published in Great Britain by Phoenix House in 1999
This paperback edition published in 1999 by Phoenix,
an imprint of Orion Books Ltd,
Orion House, 5 Upper St Martin's Lane,
London WC2H 9EA

Copyright © 1999 by Steven Millhauser

A CIP catalogue record for this book
is available from the British Library.

ISBN: 0 75380 821 8

Printed and bound in Great Britain by
The Guernsey Press Co. Ltd, Guernsey, C.I.

To Steve Stern

Contents

The knife thrower

When we learned that Hensch, the knife thrower, was stopping at our town for a single performance at eight o'clock on Saturday night, we hesitated, wondering what we felt. Hensch, the knife thrower! Did we feel like clapping our hands for joy, like leaping to our feet and bursting into smiles of anticipation? Or did we, after all, want to tighten our lips and look away in stern disapproval? That was Hensch for you. For if Hensch was an acknowledged master of his art, that difficult and faintly unsavoury art about which we knew very little, it was also true that he bore with him certain disturbing rumours, which we reproached ourselves for having failed to heed sufficiently when they appeared from time to time in the arts section of the Sunday paper.

Hensch, the knife thrower! Of course we knew his name. Everyone knew his name, as one knows the name of a famous chess player or magician. What we couldn't be sure of was what he actually did. Dimly we recalled that the skill of his throwing had brought him early attention, but that it wasn't until he had changed the rules entirely that he was taken up in a serious way. He had stepped boldly, some said recklessly, over the line never before crossed by knife throwers and had managed to make a reputation out of a disreputable thing. Some of us seemed to recall reading that in his early carnival days he had wounded an assistant badly; after a six-month retirement he had returned with his new act. It was here that he had introduced into the chaste discipline of knife throwing the idea of the artful wound, the mark of blood that was the mark of the master. We had even heard that among his followers there were many, young women especially, who longed to be wounded by the master and to bear his scar proudly. If rumours of this kind were disturbing to us, if they prevented us from celebrating Hensch's arrival with innocent delight, we nevertheless acknowledged that without such dubious enticements we'd have been unlikely to attend the performance at all, since the art of knife throwing, for all its apparent danger, is really a tame art, an outmoded art – little more than a quaint old-fashioned amusement in these times of ours. The only knife throwers any of us had ever seen were in the circus sideshow or the carnival ten-in-one, along with the fat lady and the human skeleton. It must, we imagined, have galled Hensch to feel himself a freak among freaks; he must have needed a way out. For wasn't he an artist, in his fashion? And so we admired his daring, even as we deplored his method and despised him as a vulgar showman; we questioned the rumours, tried to recall what we knew of him, interrogated ourselves relentlessly. Some of us dreamed of him: a monkey of a man in checked pants and a red hat, a stern officer in glistening boots. The promotional mailings showed only a knife held by a gloved hand. Is it surprising we didn't know what to feel?

At eight o'clock precisely, Hensch walked onto the stage: a brisk unsmiling man in black tails. His entrance surprised us. For although most of us had been seated since half-past seven, others were still arriving, moving down the aisles, pushing past half-turned knees into squeaking seats. In fact we were so accustomed to delays for latecomers that an eight o'clock performance was understood to mean one that began at 8.10 or even 8.15. As Hensch strode across the stage, a busy no-nonsense man, black-haired and top-bald, we didn't know whether we admired him for his supreme indifference to our noises of settling in, or disliked him for his refusal to countenance the slightest delay. He walked quickly across the stage to a waist-high table on which rested a mahogany box. He wore no gloves. At the opposite corner of the stage, in the rear, a black wooden partition bisected the stage walls. Hensch stepped behind his box and opened it to reveal a glitter of knives. At this moment a woman in a loose-flowing white gown stepped in front of the dark partition. Her pale hair was pulled tightly back and she carried a silver bowl.

While the latecomers among us whispered their way past knees and coats, and slipped guiltily into their seats, the woman faced us and reached into her bowl. From it she removed a white hoop about the size of a dinner plate. She held it up and turned it from side to side, as if for our inspection, while Hensch lifted from his box half a dozen knives. Then he stepped to the side of the table. He held the six knives fanwise in his left hand, with the blades pointing up. The knives were about a foot long, the blades shaped like elongated diamonds, and as he stood there at the side of the stage, a man with no expression on his face, a man with nothing to do, Hensch had the vacant and slightly bored look of an overgrown boy holding in one hand an awkward present, waiting patiently for someone to open a door.

With a gentle motion the woman in the white gown tossed the hoop lightly in the air in front of the black wooden partition. Suddenly a knife sank deep into the soft wood, catching the hoop, which hung swinging on the handle. Before we could decide whether or not to applaud, the woman tossed another white hoop. Hensch lifted and threw in a single swift smooth motion and the second hoop hung swinging from the second knife. After the third hoop rose in the air and hung suddenly on a knife handle, the woman reached into her bowl and held up for our inspection a smaller hoop, the size of a saucer. Hensch raised a knife and caught the flying hoop cleanly against the wood. She next tossed two small hoops one after the other, which Hensch caught in two swift motions: the first at the top of its trajectory, the second near the middle of the partition.

We watched Hensch as he picked up three more knives and spread them fanwise in his left hand. He stood staring at his assistant with fierce attention, his back straight, his thick hand resting by his side. When she tossed three small hoops, one after the other, we saw his body tighten, we waited for the thunk-thunk-thunk of knives in wood, but he stood immobile, sternly gazing. The hoops struck the floor, bounced slightly and began rolling like big dropped coins across the stage. Hadn't he liked the throw? We felt like looking away, like pretending we hadn't noticed. Nimbly the assistant gathered the rolling hoops, then assumed her position by the black wall. She seemed to take a deep breath before she tossed again. This time Hensch flung his three knives with extraordinary speed, and suddenly we saw all three hoops swinging on the partition, the last mere inches from the floor. She motioned grandly towards Hensch, who did not bow; we burst into vigorous applause.

Again the woman in the white gown reached into her bowl, and this time she held up something between her thumb and forefinger that even those of us in the first rows could not immediately make out. She stepped forward and many of us recognized, between her fingers, an orange and black butterfly. She returned to the partition and looked at Hensch, who had already chosen his knife. With a gentle tossing gesture she released the butterfly. We burst into applause as the knife drove the butterfly against the wood, where those in the front rows could see the wings helplessly beating.

That was something we hadn't seen before, or even imagined we might see, something worth remembering; and as we applauded we tried to recall the knife throwers of our childhood, the smell of sawdust and cotton candy, the glittering woman on the turning wheel.

Now the woman in white removed the knives from the black partition and carried them across the stage to Hensch, who examined each one closely and wiped it with a cloth before returning it to his box.

Abruptly, Hensch strode to the centre of the stage and turned to face us. His assistant pushed the table with its box of knives to his side. She left the stage and returned pushing a second table, which she placed at his other side. She stepped away, into half-darkness, while the lights shone directly on Hensch and his tables. We saw him place his left hand palm up on the empty table top. With his right hand he removed a knife from the box on the first table. Suddenly, without looking, he tossed the knife straight up into the air. We saw it rise to its rest and come hurtling down. Someone cried out as it struck his palm, but Hensch raised his hand from the table and held it up for us to see, turning it first one way and then the other: the knife had struck between the fingers. Hensch lowered his hand over the knife so that the blade stuck up between his second and third fingers. He tossed three more knives into the air, one after the other: rat-tat-tat they struck the table. From the shadows the woman in white stepped forward and tipped the table towards us, so that we could see the four knives sticking between his fingers.

Oh, we admired Hensch, we were taken with the man's fine daring; and yet, as we pounded out our applause, we felt a little restless, a little dissatisfied, as if some unspoken promise had failed to be kept. For hadn't we been a trifle ashamed of ourselves for attending the performance, hadn't we deplored in advance his unsavoury antics, his questionable crossing of the line?

As if in answer to our secret impatience, Hensch strode decisively to his corner of the stage. Quickly the pale-haired assistant followed, pushing the table after him. She next shifted the second table to the back of the stage and returned to the black partition. She stood with her back against it, gazing across the stage at Hensch, her loose white gown hanging from thin shoulder straps that had slipped down to her upper arms. At that moment we felt in our arms and along our backs a first faint flutter of anxious excitement, for there they stood before us, the dark master and the pale maiden, like figures in a dream from which we were trying to awake.

Hensch chose a knife and raised it beside his head with deliberation; we realized that he had worked very quickly before. With a swift sharp drop of his forearm, as if he were chopping a piece of wood, he released the knife. At first we thought he had struck her upper arm, but we saw that the blade had sunk into the wood and lay touching her skin. A second knife struck beside her other upper arm. She began to wriggle both shoulders, as if to free herself from the tickling knives, and only as her loose gown came rippling down did we realize that the knives had cut the shoulder straps. Hensch had us now, he had us. Long-legged and smiling, she stepped from the fallen gown and stood before the black partition in a spangled silver leotard. We thought of tightrope walkers, bareback riders, hot circus tents on blue summer days. The pale yellow hair, the spangled cloth, the pale skin touched here and there with shadow, all this gave her the remote, enclosed look of a work of art, while at the same time it lent her a kind of cool voluptuousness, for the metallic glitter of her costume seemed to draw attention to the bareness of her skin, disturbingly unhidden, dangerously white and cool and soft.

Quickly the glittering assistant stepped to the second table at the back of the stage and removed something from the drawer. She returned to the centre of the wooden partition and placed on her head a red apple. The apple was so red and shiny that it looked as if it had been painted with nail polish. We looked at Hensch, who stared at her and held himself very still. In a single motion Hensch lifted and threw. She stepped out from under the red apple stuck in the wood.

From the table she removed a second apple and clenched the stem with her teeth. At the black partition she bent slowly backwards until the bright red apple was above her upturned lips. We could see the column of her trachea pressing against the skin of her throat and the knobs of her hips pushing up against the silver spangles. Hensch took careful aim and flung the knife through the heart of the apple.

Next from the table she removed a pair of long white gloves, which she pulled on slowly, turning her wrists, tugging. She held up each tight-gloved hand in turn and wriggled the fingers. At the partition she stood with her arms out and her fingers spread. Hensch looked at her, then raised a knife and threw; it stuck into her fingertip, the middle fingertip of her right hand, pinning her to the black wall. The woman stared straight ahead. Hensch picked up a clutch of knives and held them fanwise in his left hand. Swiftly he flung nine knives, one after the other, and as they struck her fingertips, one after the other, bottom to top, right-left right-left, we stirred uncomfortably in our seats. In the sudden silence she stood there with her arms outspread and her fingers full of knives, her silver spangles flashing, her white gloves whiter than her pale arms, looking as if at any moment her head would drop forward – looking for all the world like a martyr on a cross. Then slowly, gently, she pulled each hand from its glove, leaving the gloves hanging on the wall.

Now Hensch gave a sharp wave of his fingers, as if to dismiss everything that had gone before, and to our surprise the woman stepped forward to the edge of the stage and addressed us for the first time.

'I must ask you', she said gently, 'to be very quiet, because this next act is very dangerous. The master will mark me. Please do not make a sound. We thank you.'

She returned to the black partition and simply stood there, her shoulders back, her arms down but pressed against the wood. She gazed steadily at Hensch, who seemed to be studying her; some of us said later that at this moment she gave the impression of a child who was about to be struck in the face, though others felt she looked calm, quite calm.

Hensch chose a knife from his box, held it for a moment, then raised his arm and threw. The knife struck beside her neck. He had missed – had he missed? – and we felt a sharp tug of disappointment, which changed at once to shame, deep shame, for we hadn't come out for blood, only for – well, something else; and as we asked ourselves what we had come for, we were surprised to see her reach up with one hand and pull out the knife. Then we saw, on her neck, the thin red trickle, which ran down to her shoulder; and we understood that her whiteness had been arranged for this moment. Long and loud we applauded, as she bowed and held aloft the glittering knife, assuring us, in that way, that she was wounded but well, or well-wounded; and we didn't know whether we were applauding her wellness or her wound, or the touch of the master, who had crossed the line, who had carried us, safely, it appeared, into the realm of forbidden things.

Even as we applauded she turned and left the stage, returning a few moments later in a long black dress with long sleeves and a high collar, which concealed her wound. We imagined the white bandage under the black collar; we imagined other bandages, other wounds, on her hips, her waist, the edges of her breasts. Black against black they stood there, she and he, bound now it seemed in a dark pact, as if she were his twin sister, or as if both were on the same side in a game we were all playing, a game we no longer understood; and indeed she looked older in her black dress, sterner, a schoolmarm or maiden aunt. We were not surprised when she stepped forward to address us again.

'If any of you, in the audience, wish to be marked by the master, to receive the mark of the master, now is the time. Is there anyone?'

We all looked around. A single hand rose hesitantly and was instantly lowered. Another hand went up; then there were other hands, young bodies straining forward, eager; and from the stage the woman in black descended and walked slowly along an aisle, looking closely, considering, until she stopped and pointed: 'You.' And we knew her, Susan Parker, a high-school girl, who might have been our daughter, sitting there with her face turned questioningly towards the woman, her eyebrows slightly raised, as she pointed to herself; then the faint flush of realization; and as she climbed the steps of the stage we watched her closely, wondering what the dark woman had seen in her, to make her be the one, wondering too what she was thinking, Susan Parker, as she followed the dark woman to the wooden partition. She was wearing loose jeans and a tight black short-sleeved sweater; her reddish-brown and faintly shiny hair was cut short. Was it for her white skin she had been chosen? or some air of self-possession? We wanted to cry out: sit down! you don't have to do this! but we remained silent, respectful. Hensch stood at his table, watching without expression. It occurred to us that we trusted him at this moment; we clung to him; he was all we had; for if we weren't absolutely sure of him, then who were we, what on earth were we, who had allowed things to come to such a pass?

The woman in black led Susan Parker to the wooden partition and arranged her there: back to the wood, shoulders straight. We saw her run her hand gently, as if tenderly, over the girl's short hair, which lifted and fell back in place. Then taking Susan

Parker's right hand in hers, she stepped to the girl's right, so that the entire arm was extended against the black partition. She stood holding Susan Parker's raised hand, gazing at the girl's face – comforting her, it seemed; and we observed that Susan Parker's arm looked very white between the black sweater and the black dress, against the black wood of the partition. As the women gazed at each other, Hensch lifted a knife and threw. We heard the muffled bang of the blade, heard Susan Parker's sharp little gasp, saw her other hand clench into a fist. Quickly the dark woman stepped in front of her and pulled out the knife; and turning to us she lifted Susan Parker's arm, and displayed for us a streak of red on the pale forearm. Then she reached into a pocket of her black dress and removed a small tin box. From the box came a ball of cotton, a patch of gauze and a roll of white surgical tape, with which she swiftly bound the wound. 'There, dear,' we heard her say. 'You were very brave.' We watched Susan Parker walk with lowered eyes across the stage, holding her bandaged arm a little away from her body; and as we began to clap, because she was still there, because she had come through, we saw her raise her eyes and give a quick shy smile, before lowering her lashes and descending the steps.

Now arms rose, seats creaked, there was a great rustling and whispering among us, for others were eager to be chosen, to be marked by the master, and once again the woman in black stepped forward to speak.

'Thank you, dear. You were very brave, and now you will bear the mark of the master. You will treasure it all your days. But it is a light mark, do you know, a very light mark. The master can mark more deeply, far more deeply. But for that you must show yourself worthy. Some of you may already be worthy, but I will ask you now to lower your hands, please, for I have with me someone who is ready to be marked. And please, all of you, I ask for your silence.'

From the right of the stage stepped forth a young man who

might have been fifteen or sixteen. He was dressed in black pants and a black shirt and wore rimless glasses that caught the light. He carried himself with ease, and we saw that he had a kind of lanky and slightly awkward beauty, the beauty, we thought, of a waterbird, a heron. The woman led him to the wooden partition and indicated that he should stand with his back against it. She walked to the table at the rear of the stage and removed an object, which she carried back to the partition. Raising the boy's left arm, so that it was extended straight out against the wall at the level of his shoulder, she lifted the object to his wrist and began fastening it into the wood. It appeared to be a clamp, which held his arm in place at the wrist. She then arranged his hand: palm facing us, fingers together. Stepping away, she looked at him thoughtfully. Then she stepped over to his free side, took his other hand and held it gently.

The stage lights went dark, then a reddish spotlight shone on Hensch at his box of knives. A second light, white as moonlight, shone on the boy and his extended arm. The other side of the boy remained in darkness.

Even as the performance seemed to taunt us with the promise of danger, of a disturbing turn that should not be permitted, or even imagined, we reminded ourselves that the master had so far done nothing but scratch a bit of skin, that his act was after all public and well travelled, that the boy appeared calm; and though we disapproved of the exaggerated effect of the lighting, the crude melodrama of it all, we secretly admired the skill with which the performance played on our fears. What it was we feared, exactly, we didn't know, couldn't say. But there was the knife thrower bathed in blood-light, there was the pale victim manacled to a wall; in the shadows the dark woman; and in the glare of the lighting, in the silence, in the very rhythm of the evening, the promise of entering a dark dream.

And Hensch took up a knife and threw; some heard the sharp gasp of the boy, others a thin cry. In the whiteness of the light we saw the knife handle at the centre of his bloody palm. Some said that at the moment the knife struck, the boy's shocked face shone with an intense, almost painful joy. The white light suddenly illuminated the woman in black, who raised his free arm high, as if in triumph; then she quickly set to work pulling out the blade, wrapping the palm in strips of gauze, wiping the boy's drained and sweating face with a cloth, and leading him off the stage with an arm firmly around his waist. No one made a sound. We looked at Hensch, who was gazing after his assistant.

When she came back, alone, she stepped forward to address us, while the stage lights returned to normal.

'You are a brave boy, Thomas. You will not soon forget this day. And now I must say that we have time for only one more event, this evening. Many of you here, I know, would like to receive the palm mark, as Thomas did. But I am asking something different now. Is there anyone in this audience tonight who would like to make' – and here she paused, not hesitantly, but as if in emphasis – 'the ultimate sacrifice? This is the final mark, the mark that can be received only once. Please think it over carefully, before raising your hand.'

We wanted her to say more, to explain clearly what it was she meant by those riddling words, which came to us as though whispered in our ears, in the dark, words that seemed to mock us even as they eluded us – and we looked about tensely, almost eagerly, as if by the sheer effort of our looking we were asserting our vigilance. We saw no hands, and maybe it was true that at the very centre of our relief there was a touch of disappointment, but it was relief none the less; and if the entire performance had seemed to be leading towards some overwhelming moment that was no longer to take place, still we had been entertained by our knife thrower, had we not, we had been carried a long way, so that even as we questioned his cruel art we were ready to offer our applause.

'If there are no hands,' she said, looking at us sharply, as if to see what it was we were secretly thinking, while we, as if to avoid her gaze, looked rapidly all about. 'Oh: yes?' We saw it too, the partly raised hand, which perhaps had always been there, unseen in the half-darkened seats, and we saw the stranger rise and begin to make her way slowly past drawn-in knees and pulled-back coats and half-risen forms. We watched her climb the steps of the stage, a tall mournful-looking girl in jeans and a dark blouse, with lank long hair and slouched shoulders. 'And what is your name?' the woman in black said gently, and we could not hear the answer. 'Well then, Laura. And so you are prepared to receive the final mark? Then you must be very brave.' And turning to us she said, 'I must ask you, please, to remain absolutely silent.'

She led the girl to the black wooden partition and arranged her there, unconfined: chin up, hands hanging awkwardly at her sides. The dark woman stepped back and appeared to assess her arrangement, after which she crossed to the back of the stage. At this point some of us had confused thoughts of calling out, of demanding an explanation, but we didn't know what it was we might be protesting, and in any case the thought of distracting Hensch's throw, of perhaps causing an injury, was repellent to us, for we saw that already he had selected a knife. It was a new kind of knife, or so we thought, a longer and thinner knife. And it seemed to us that things were happening too quickly, up there on the stage, for where was the spotlight, where was the drama of a sudden darkening, but Hensch, even as we wondered, did what he always did – he threw his knife. Some of us heard the girl cry out, others were struck by her silence, but what stayed with all of us was the absence of the sound of the knife striking wood. Instead there was a softer sound, a more disturbing sound, a sound almost like silence, and some said the girl looked down, as if in surprise. Others claimed to see in her face, in the expression of her eyes, a look of rapture. As she fell to the floor the dark woman stepped forward and swept her arm towards the knife thrower, who for the first time turned to acknowledge us. And now he bowed: a deep, slow, graceful bow, the bow of a master, down to his knees. Slowly the dark red curtain began to fall. Overhead the lights came on.

As we left the theatre we agreed that it had been a skilful performance, though we couldn't help feeling that the knife thrower had gone too far. He had justified his reputation, of that there could be no question; without ever trying to ingratiate himself with us, he had continually seized our deepest attention. But for all that, we couldn't help feeling that he ought to have found some other way. Of course the final act had probably been a set-up, the girl had probably leaped smiling to her feet as soon as the curtain closed, though some of us recalled unpleasant rumours of one kind or another, run-ins with the police, charges and countercharges, a murky business. In any case we reminded ourselves that she hadn't been coerced in any way, none of them had been coerced in any way. And it was certainly true that a man in Hensch's position had every right to improve his art, to dream up new acts with which to pique curiosity, indeed such advances were absolutely necessary, for without them a knife thrower could never hope to keep himself in the public eye. Like the rest of us, he had to earn his living, which admittedly wasn't easy in times like these. But when all was said and done, when the pros and cons were weighed and every issue carefully considered, we couldn't help feeling that the knife thrower had really gone too far. After all, if such performances were encouraged, if they were even tolerated, what might we expect in the future? Would any of us be safe? The more we thought about it, the more uneasy we became, and in the nights that followed, when we woke from troubling dreams, we remembered the travelling knife thrower with agitation and dismay.

A visit

Although I had not heard from my friend in nine years, I wasn't surprised, not really, to receive a short letter from him dashed off in pencil, announcing that he had 'taken a wife' and summoning me to visit him in some remote upstate town I had never heard of. 'Come see me on the 16th and 17th' was what he had actually written. 'Be here for lunch.' The offhand peremptory tone was Albert all over. He had scribbled a map, with a little black circle marked 'Village' and a little white square marked 'My house'. A wavy line connected the two. Under the line were the words '3½ miles, more or less'. Over the line were the words 'County Road 39'. I knew those desolate little upstate villages, consisting of one Baptist church, three bars and a gas station with a single pump, and I imagined Albert living at an ironic distance, with his books and his manias. What I couldn't imagine was his wife. Albert had never struck me as the marrying kind, though women had always liked him. I had plans for the weekend, but I cancelled them and headed north.

I still considered Albert my friend, in a way my best friend, even though I hadn't heard from him in nine years. He had once been my best friend and it was hard to think of him in any other way. Even in the flourishing time of our friendship, in the last two years of college and the year after, when we saw each other daily, he had been a difficult and exacting friend, scornful of convention though quiet in his own habits, subject to sudden flare-ups and silences, earnest but with an edge of mockery, intolerant of mediocrity and cursed with an unfailing scent for the faintly fraudulent in a gesture or a phrase or a face. He was handsome in a sharp-featured New England way – his family, as he put it, had lived in Connecticut since the fall of the Roman Empire – but despite the inviting smiles of girls in his classes he confined himself to brisk affairs with leather-jacketed town girls with whom he had nothing in common. After graduating, we roomed together for a year in a little college town full of cafés and bookstores, sharing the rent and drifting from one part-time job to another, as I put off the inevitable suit-and-tie life that awaited me while he mocked my conventional fear of becoming conventional, defended business as America's only source of originality, and read his Plato and his *Modern Chess Openings* and tootled his flute. One day he left, just like that, to start what he called a new life. In the next year I received postcards from small towns all over America, showing pictures of Main Streets and quaint village railroad stations. They bore messages such as 'Still looking' or 'Have you seen my razor? I think I left it on the bathtub'. Then there was nothing for six months, and then a sudden postcard from Eugene, Oregon, on which he described in minute detail a small unknown wooden object that he had found in the top drawer of the bureau in his rented bedroom, and then nine years of silence. During that time I had settled into a job and almost married an old girlfriend. I had bought a house on a pleasant street lined with porches and maples, thought quite a bit about my old friend Albert and wondered whether this was what I had looked forward to, this life I was now leading, in the old days, the days when I still looked forward to things.

The town was even worse than I had imagined. Slowly I

passed its crumbling brick paper mill with boarded-up windows, its rows of faded and flaking two-family houses with sagging front porches where guys in black T-shirts sat drinking beer, its tattoo parlour and its sluggish stream. County Road 39 wound between fields of Queen Anne's lace and yellow ragweed, with now and then a melancholy house or a patch of sun-scorched corn. Once I passed a rotting barn with a caved-in roof. At 3.2 miles on the odometer I came to a weathered house near the edge of the road. A bicycle lay in the high grass of the front yard and an open garage was entirely filled with old furniture. Uncertainly I turned onto the unpaved drive, parked with the motor running and walked up to the front door. There was no bell. I knocked on the wooden screen door, which banged loudly against the frame, and a tall, barefoot and very pale woman with sleepy eyes came to the door, wearing a long rumpled black skirt and a lumberjack shirt over a T-shirt. When I asked for Albert she looked at me suspiciously, shook her head quickly twice and slammed the inner door. As I walked back to the car I saw her pale face looking out at me past a pushed-aside pink curtain. It occurred to me that perhaps Albert had married this woman and that she was insane. It further occurred to me, as I backed out of the drive, that I really ought to turn back now, right now, away from this misguided adventure in the wilderness. After all, I hadn't seen him for nine long years, things were bound to be different. At 4.1 miles on the odometer I rounded a bend of rising road and saw a shadowy house set back in a cluster of dusty-looking trees. I turned in to the unknown dirt drive, deep-rutted and sprouting weeds, and as I stepped on the brake with a sharp sense of desolation and betrayal, for here I was, in the godforsaken middle of nauseating nowhere, prowling around like a fool and a criminal, the front door opened and Albert came out, one hand in his pocket and one hand waving.

He looked the same, nearly the same, though browner and leatherier than I remembered, as if he had lived all those years in the sun, his face a little longer and leaner – a handsome man in jeans and a dark shirt. 'I wondered if you'd show up,' he said when he reached the car, and suddenly seemed to study me. 'You look just the way you ought to,' he then said.

I let the words settle in me. 'It depends what I ought to look like,' I answered, glancing at him sharply, but he only laughed.

'Isn't this a great place?' he said, throwing out one arm as he began carrying my travelling bag towards the house. 'Ten acres and they're practically giving it away. First day after I bought the place I go walking around and bingo! what do you think I found? Grapes. Billions of grapes. An old fallen-down grape arbour, grapes growing all over the ground. Italy in New York. Wait till you see the pond.'

We stepped into the shade of the high trees, a little thicket of pines and maples, that grew close to the house. Big bushes climbed half-way up the windows. It struck me that the house was well protected from view, a private place, a shadowy isle in a sea of fields. 'And yet,' I said, looking around for his wife, 'somehow I never thought of you as getting married, somehow.'

'Not back then,' he said. 'Watch that rail.'

We had climbed onto the steps of the long, deep-shaded front porch and I had grasped a wobbly iron handrail that needed to be screwed into the wood. A coil of old garden hose hung over the porch rail. A few hornets buzzed about the ceiling light. On the porch stood a sunken *chaise longue*, an old three-speed bicycle, a metal garbage can containing a rusty snow shovel and a porch swing on which sat an empty flowerpot.

He opened the wooden screen door and with a little flourish urged me in. 'Humble,' he said, 'but mine own.' He looked at me with a kind of excitement, an excitement I couldn't entirely account for, but which reminded me of the old excitement, and I wondered, as I entered the house, whether that was what I had been looking for, back then. The house was cool and almost dark, the dark of deep shade lightened by streaks of sun. Under the half-drawn window shades I saw bush-branches growing against the glass. We had entered the living-room, where I noticed a rocking chair that leaned too far back and a couch with one pillow. Ancient wallpaper showed faded scenes of some kind repeating themselves all over the room. Albert, who seemed more and more excited, led me up the creaking worn-edged stairs to my room – a bed with a frilly pink spread, a lamp table on which lay a screwdriver with a transparent yellow handle – and quickly back down.

'You must be starving,' he said, with that odd quiver of excitement, as he led me through an open doorway into a dining-room that was almost dark. At a big round table there were three place settings, which glowed whitely in the gloom. One of the round-backed chairs appeared to be occupied. Only as I drew closer through the afternoon darkness did I see that the occupant was a large frog, perhaps two feet high, which sat with its throat resting on the table edge. 'My wife,' Albert said, looking at me fiercely, as if he were about to spring at my face. I felt I was being tested in some fiendish way. 'Pleased to meet you,' I said harshly and sat down across from her. The table lay between us like a lake. I had thought she might be something else, maybe a stuffed toy of some sort, but even in the dark daylight I could see the large moist eyes looking here and there, I could see her rapid breathing and smell her marshy odour. I thought Albert must be making fun of me in some fashion, trying to trick me into exposing what he took to be my hideous bourgeois soul, but whatever his game I wasn't going to give myself away.

'Help yourself,' Albert said, pushing towards me a breadboard with a round loaf and a hunk of cheese on it. A big-bladed knife lay on the table and I began cutting the bread. 'And if you'd cut just a little piece of cheese for Alice.' I immediately cut a little piece of cheese for Alice. Albert disappeared into the kitchen and in the room's dusk I stared across the round table at Alice

before looking away uncomfortably. Albert returned with a wax
carton of orange juice and a small brown bottle of beer, both of
which he set before me. 'The choice', he said with a little bow,
'is yours entirely.' He picked up the piece of cheese I had cut for
Alice, placed it on her plate and broke it into smaller pieces.
Alice looked at him – it seemed to me that she looked at him –
with those moist and heavy-lidded eyes, and flicked up her
cheese. Then she placed her throat on the table edge and sat
very still.

Albert sat down and cut himself a piece of bread. 'After lunch
I want to show you the place. Take you down to the pond and
so on.' He looked at me, tilting his head in a way I suddenly
remembered. 'And you? It's been a while.'

'Oh, still a roving bachelor,' I said, and immediately disliked
my fatuous tone. I had a sudden urge to talk seriously to Albert,
as we'd done in the old days, watching the night turn slowly
grey through our tall, arched windows. But I felt constrained, it
had been too long a time, and though he had summoned me
after all these years, though he had shown me his wife, it was all
askew somehow, as if he hadn't shown me anything, as if he'd
kept himself hidden away. And I remembered that even then, in
the time of our friendship, he had seemed intimate and
secretive at the same time, as if even his revelations were forms
of concealment. 'Not that I have any fixed plan,' I continued. 'I
see women, but they're not the right one. You know, I was
always sure I'd be the one to get married, not you.'

'It wasn't something I planned. But when the moment
comes, you'll know.' He looked at Alice with tenderness and
suddenly leaned over and touched the side of her head lightly
with his fingertips.

'How did you,' I began, and stopped. I felt like bursting into
screams of wild laughter, or of outrage, pure outrage, but I held
myself down, I pretended everything was fine. 'I mean, how did
you meet? You two. If I may ask.'

'So formal! If you may ask! Down by the pond – if I may answer. I saw her in the reeds one day. I'd never seen her before, but she was always there, after that. I'll show you the exact place after lunch.'

His little mocking rebuke irritated me and I recalled how he had always irritated me, and made me retreat more deeply into myself, because of some little reproach, some little ironic look, and it seemed strange to me that someone who irritated me and made me retreat into myself was also someone who released me into a freer version of myself, a version superior to the constricted one that had always felt like my own hand on my throat. But who was Albert, after all, that he should have the power to release me or constrict me – this man I no longer knew, with his run-down house and his ludicrous frog-wife. Then I ate for a while in sullen silence, looking only at my food, and when I glanced up I saw him looking at me kindly, almost affectionately.

'It's all right,' he said quietly, as if he understood, as if he knew how difficult it was for me, this journey, this wife, this life. And I was grateful, as I had always been, for we had been close, he and I, back then.

After lunch he insisted on showing me his land – his domain, as he called it. I had hoped that Alice might stay behind, so that I could speak with him alone, but it was clear that he wanted her to come with us. So as we made our way out the back door and into his domain she followed along, taking hops about two strides in length, always a little behind us or a little before. At the back of the house a patch of overgrown lawn led to a vegetable garden on both sides of a grassy path. There were vines of green peas and string-beans climbing tall sticks, clusters of green peppers, rows of carrots and radishes identified by seed packets on short sticks, fat heads of lettuce and flashes of yellow squash – a rich and well-tended oasis, as if the living centre of the house were here, on the outside, hidden in back. At the end of the garden grew a scattering of fruit trees, pear and cherry and plum. An old wire fence with a broken wooden gate separated the garden from the land beyond.

We walked along a vague footpath through fields of high grass, passed into thickets of oak and maple, crossed a stream. Alice kept up the pace. Alice in sunlight, Alice in the open air, no longer seemed a grotesque pet, a monstrous mistake of Nature, a nightmare frog and freakish wife, but rather a companion of sorts, staying alongside us, resting when we rested – Albert's pal. And yet it was more than that. For when she emerged from high grass or treeshade into full sunlight, I saw or sensed for a moment, with a kind of inner start, Alice as she was, Alice in the sheer brightness and fullness of her being, as if the dark malachite sheen of her skin, the pale shimmer of her throat, the moist warmth of her eyes, were as natural and mysterious as the flight of a bird. Then I would tumble back into myself and realize that I was walking with my old friend beside a monstrous lumbering frog who had somehow become his wife, and a howl of inward laughter and rage would erupt in me, calmed almost at once by the rolling meadows, the shady thickets, the black crow rising from a tree with slowly lifted and lowered wings, rising higher and higher into the pale blue sky touched here and there with delicate fernlike clouds.

The pond appeared suddenly, on the far side of a low rise. Reeds and cat's-tails grew in thick clusters at the marshy edge. We sat down on flat-topped boulders and looked out at the green-brown water, where a few brown ducks floated, out past fields to a line of low hills. There was a desolate beauty about the place, as if we had come to the edge of the world. 'It was over there I first saw her,' Albert said, pointing to a cluster of reeds. Alice sat off to one side, low to the ground, in a clump of grass at the water's edge. She was still as a rock, except for her sides moving in and out as she breathed. I imagined her growing in the depths of the pond, under a mantle of lilypads and mottled scum, down below the rays of green sunlight, far down, at the silent bottom of the world.

Albert leaned back on both elbows, a pose I remembered well, and stared out at the water. For a long while we sat in a silence that struck me as uncomfortable, though he himself seemed at ease. It wasn't so much that I felt awkward in Alice's presence as that I didn't know what I had come all this way to say. Did I really want to speak at all? Then Albert said, 'Tell me about your life.' And I was grateful to him, for that was exactly what I wanted to talk about, my life. I told him about my almost-marriage, my friendships that lacked excitement, my girlfriends who lacked one thing or another, my good job that somehow wasn't exactly what I had been looking for, back then, my feeling that things were all right but not as all right as they might be, that I was not unhappy but not really happy either, but caught in some intermediate place, looking both ways. And as I spoke it seemed to me that I was looking in one direction towards a happiness that was growing vaguer and in the other direction towards an unhappiness that was emerging more clearly, without yet revealing itself completely.

'It's hard,' Albert then said, in the tone of someone who knew what I was talking about, and though I was soothed by his words, which were spoken gently, I was disappointed that he didn't say more, that he didn't show himself to me.

And I said, 'Why did you write to me, after all this time?' which was only another way of saying, why didn't you write to me, in all this time.

'I waited', he said, 'until I had something to show you.' That was what he said: something to show me. And it seemed to me then that if all he had to show me after nine years was his run-down house and his marshy frog-wife, then I wasn't so badly off, in my own way, not really.

After that we continued walking about his domain, with Alice always at our side. He showed me things and I looked. He showed me the old grape arbour that he had put back up; unripe green grapes, hard as nuts, hung in bunches from the decaying slats. 'Try one,' he said, but it was bitter as a tiny lemon. He laughed at my grimace. 'We like 'em this way,' he said, plucking a few into his palm, then tossing them into his mouth. He pulled off another handful and held them down to Alice, who devoured them swiftly: flick flick flick. He showed me a woodpecker's nest and a slope of wild tiger lilies, and an old toolshed containing a rusty hoe and a rusty rake. Suddenly, from a nearby field, a big bird rose up with a loud beating of wings. 'Did you see that!' cried Albert, seizing my arm. 'A pheasant! Protecting her young. Over there.' In the high grass six fuzzy little ducklike creatures walked in a line, their heads barely visible.

At dinner Alice sat in her chair with her throat resting on the edge of the table while Albert walked briskly in and out of the kitchen. I was pleased to see a fat bottle of red wine, which he poured into two juice glasses. The glasses had pictures of Winnie-the-Pooh and Eeyore on them. 'Guy gave them to me at a gas station,' Albert said. He frowned suddenly, pressed his fingertips against his forehead, looked up with a radiant smile. 'I've got it. The more it *snows*, tiddely-pom, the more it *goes*, tiddely-pom.' He poured a little wine into a cereal bowl and placed it near Alice.

Dinner was a heated-up supermarket chicken, fresh squash from his garden and big bowls of garden salad. Albert was in high spirits, humming snatches of songs, lighting a stub of candle in a green wine bottle, filling our wineglasses and Alice's bowl again and again, urging me to drink up, crunching lustily into his salad. The cheap wine burned my tongue but I kept drinking, taken by Albert's festive spirit, eager to carry myself into his mood. Even Alice kept finishing the wine he put in her cereal bowl. The candle flame seemed to grow brighter in the darkening air of the room; through bush-branches in the window I saw streaks of sunset. A line of wax ran down the bottle and stopped. Albert brought in his breadboard, more salad, another loaf of bread. And as the meal continued I had the sense that Alice, sitting there with her throat resting on the table edge, flicking up her wine, was looking at Albert with those large eyes of hers, moist and dark in the flame light. She was looking at him and trying to attract his attention. Albert was leaning back in his chair, laughing, throwing his arm about as he talked, but it seemed to me that he was darting glances back at her. Yes, they were exchanging looks, there at the darkening dinner-table, looks that struck me as amorous. And as I drank I was filled with a warm, expansive feeling, which took in the room, the meal, the Winnie-the-Pooh glasses, the large moist eyes, the reflection of the candle flame in the black window, the glances of Albert and his wife; for after all, she was the one he had chosen, up here in the wilderness, and who was I to say what was right, in such matters.

Albert leaped up and returned with a bowl of pears and cherries from his fruit trees, and filled my glass again. I was settling back with my warm, expansive feeling, looking forward to the night of talk stretching lazily before me, when Albert announced that it was getting late, he and Alice would be retiring. I had the run of the house. Just be sure to blow out the candle. Nighty night. Through the roar of wine I was aware of my plunging disappointment. He pulled back her chair and she hopped to the floor. Together they left the dining-room and disappeared into the dark living-room, where he turned on a lamp so dim that it was like lighting a candle. I heard him creaking up the stairs and thought I heard a dull thumping sound, as I imagined Alice lumbering her way up beside him.

I sat listening to the thumps and creaks of the upper hall, a sudden sharp rush of water in the bathroom sink, a squeak – what was that squeak? – a door shutting. In the abrupt silence, which seemed to spread outwards from the table in widening ripples, I felt abandoned, there with the wine and the candle and the glimmering dishes. Yet I saw that it was bound to be this way and no other way, for I had watched their amorous looks, it was only to be expected. And hadn't he, back then, been in the habit of unexpected departures? Then I began to wonder whether they had ever taken place, those talks stretching into the grey light of dawn, or whether I had only desired them. Then I imagined Alice hopping onto the white sheets. And I tried to imagine frog-love, its possible pleasures, its oozy raptures, but I turned my mind violently away, for in the imagining I felt something petty and cruel, something in the nature of a violation.

I drank down the last of the wine and blew out the candle. From the dark room where I sat I could see a ghostly corner of refrigerator in the kitchen and a dim-lit reddish couch-arm in the living-room, like a moonlit dead flower. A car passed on the road. Then I became aware of the crickets, whole fields and meadows of them, the great hum that I had always heard rising from backyards and vacant lots in childhood summers, the long sound of summer's end. And yet it was only the middle of summer, was it not, just last week I had spent a day at the beach. So for a long time I sat at the dark table, in the middle of a decaying house, listening to the sound of summer's end. Then I picked up my empty glass, silently saluted Albert and his wife, and went up to bed.

But I could not sleep. Maybe it was the wine, or the mashed mattress, or the early hour, but I lay there twisting in my sheets, and as I turned restlessly, the day's adventures darkened in my mind and I saw only a crazed friend, a ruined house, an ugly and monstrous frog. And I saw myself, weak and absurd, wrenching my mind into grotesque shapes of sympathy and understanding. At some point I began to slide in and out of dreams, or perhaps it was a single long dream broken by many half-wakings. I was walking down a long hall with a forbidden door at the end. With a sense of mournful excitement I opened the door and saw Albert standing with his arms crossed, looking at me sternly. He began to shout at me, his face became very red, and bending over he bit me on the hand. Tears ran down my face. Behind him someone rose from a chair and came towards us. 'Here,' said the newcomer, who was somehow Albert, 'use this.' He held up a handkerchief draped over his fist, and when I pulled off the handkerchief a big frog rose angrily into the air with wild flappings of its wings.

I woke tense and exhausted in a sun-streaked room. Through a dusty window I saw tree branches with big three-lobed leaves and between the leaves pieces of blue sky. It was nearly nine. I had three separate headaches: one behind my left eye, one in my right temple and one at the back of my head. I washed and dressed quickly, and made my way down the darkening stairs, through a dusk that deepened as I drew towards the bottom. On the faded wallpaper I could make out two scenes repeating themselves into the distance: a faded boy in blue lying against a faded yellow haystack with a horn at his side, and a girl in white drawing water from a faded well.

The living-room was empty. The whole house appeared to be deserted. On the round table in the twilight of the dining-room the dishes still sat from dinner. All I wanted was a cup of coffee before leaving. In the slightly less gloomy kitchen I found an old jar of instant coffee and a chipped blue teapot decorated with a little decal picturing an orange brontosaurus. I heard sharp sounds, and through the leaves and branches in the kitchen window I saw Albert with his back to me, digging in the garden. Outside the house it was a bright, sunny day. Beside him, on the dirt, sat Alice.

I brought my cup of harsh-tasting, stale coffee into the dining-room and drank it at the table while I listened to the sounds of Albert's shovel striking the soil. It was peaceful in the darkish room, at the round brown table. A thin slant of sun glittered in the open kitchen. The sun-slant mingled with the whistle of a bird, leaves in the window, the brown dusk, the sound of the shovel striking loam, turning it over. It occurred to me that I could simply pack my things now and glide away without the awkwardness of a leave-taking.

I finished the dismal coffee and carried the cup into the kitchen, where the inner back door stood slightly open. There I paused, holding the empty cup in my hand. Obeying a sudden impulse, I opened the door a little more and slipped between it and the wooden screen door.

Through the buckled screen I could see Albert some ten feet away. His sleeves were rolled up and his foot was pressing down on the blade of the shovel. He was digging up grassy dirt at the edge of the garden, turning it over, breaking up the soil, tossing away clumps of grass roots. Nearby sat Alice, watching him. From time to time, as he moved along the edge of the garden, he would look over at her. Their looks seemed to catch for a moment, before he returned to his garden. Standing in the warm shade of the half-open door, looking through the rippling screen at the garden quivering with sunlight, I sensed a mysterious rhythm trembling between Albert and his wife, a kind of lightness or buoyancy, a quivering sunlit harmony. It was as if both of them had shed their skins and were mingling in air, or dissolving into light – and as I felt that airy mingling, that tender dissolution, as I sensed that hidden harmony, clear as the ringing of a distant bell, it came over me that what I lacked, in my life, was exactly that harmony. It was as if I were composed of some hard substance that could never dissolve in anything, whereas Albert had discovered the secret of air. But my throat was beginning to hurt, the bright light burned my eyes and, setting down my cup on the counter, which sounded like the blow of a hammer, I pushed open the door and went out.

Albert turned around in the sun. 'Sleep well?' he said, running the back of his hand slowly across his dripping forehead.

'Well enough. But you know, I've got to be getting back. A million things to do! You know how it is.'

'Sure,' Albert said. He rested both hands on the top of the long shovel handle and placed his chin on his hands. 'I know how it is.' His tone struck me as brilliantly poised between understanding and mockery.

He brought my bag down from my room and loaded it in the car. Alice had hopped through the dining-room and living-room and had come to rest in the deep shade of the front porch. It struck me that she kept carefully out of sight of the road. Albert bent over the driver's window and crossed his arms on the door. 'If you're ever up this way,' he said, but who would ever be up that way, 'drop in.' 'I'll do that,' I said. Albert stood up and stretched out an elbow, rubbed his shoulder. 'Take care,' he said, and gave a little wave and stepped away.

As I backed up the dirt driveway and began edging onto County Road 39, I had the sense that the house was withdrawing into its trees and shadows, fading into its island of shade. Albert had already vanished. From the road I could see only a stand of high trees clustered about a dark house. A few moments later, at the bend of the road, I glanced back again. I must have waited a second too long, because the road was already dipping, the house had sunk out of sight and in the bright sunshine I saw only a scattering of roadside trees, a cloudless sky, fields of Queen Anne's lace stretching away.

The sisterhood of night

What we know

In an atmosphere of furious accusation and hysterical rumour, an atmosphere in which hearsay and gossip have so thoroughly replaced the careful assessment of evidence that impartiality itself seems of the devil's party, it may be useful to adopt a calmer tone and to state what it is that we actually know. We know that the girls are between twelve and fifteen years old. We know that they travel in bands of five or six, although smaller and larger bands, ranging from two to nine, have occasionally been sighted. We know that they leave and return only at night. We know that they seek dark and secret places, such as abandoned houses, church cellars, graveyards and the woods at the north end of town. We know, or believe we know, that they have taken a vow of silence.

What we say

It is said that the girls remove their shirts and dance wild dances under the summer moon. It is said that the girls paint their breasts with snakes and strange symbols. They excite one another by brushing their breasts against the breasts of other girls, it is said. We hear that the girls drink the warm blood of murdered animals. People say that the girls engage in witchcraft, in unnatural sexual acts, in torture, in black magic, in disgusting acts of desecration. Older girls, it is said, lure young girls into the sisterhood and corrupt them. Rumour has it that the girls are instructed to carry weapons: pins, scissors, jackknives, needles, kitchen knives. It is said that the girls have vowed to kill any member who attempts to leave the sisterhood. We have heard that the girls drink a whitish liquid that makes them fall into an erotic frenzy.

The confession of Emily Gehring

Rumours of a secret society had reached us from time to time, but we paid little attention to them until the confession of thirteen-year-old Emily Gehring, who on 2 June released to the *Town Reporter* a disturbing letter. In it she stated that on 14 May, at 4 p.m., she had been contacted on the playground of David Johnson Junior High by Mary Warren, a high-school sophomore who sometimes played basketball with the younger girls. Mary Warren slipped into her hand a small piece of white paper, folded in half. When Emily Gehring opened it, she saw that one of the inner sides was entirely black. Emily felt excited and frightened, for this was the sign of the Sisterhood of Night, an obscure, impenetrable secret society much discussed on the playgrounds, at the lockers and in the bathrooms of David Johnson Junior High. She was told to speak to no one and to appear alone at midnight in the parking lot behind the Presbyterian Church. Emily Gehring stated that when she appeared at the parking lot she at first saw no one but was then met by three girls, who had slipped out of hiding places: Mary Warren, Isabel Robbins and Laura Lindberg. The girls led her through the church parking lot, along quiet roads and through backyards to the woods at the north end of town, where three other girls met them: Catherine Anderson, Hilda Meyer and Lavinia Hall. Mary Warren then asked her whether she liked boys. When she said yes, the girls mocked her and laughed at her, as if she had said something stupid. Mary Warren then asked her to remove her shirt. When she refused, the girls threatened to tie her to a tree and stick pins in her. She removed her shirt and the girls all fondled her breasts, touching them and kissing them. She then was invited to touch the breasts of the other girls; when she refused, they seized her hands and forced her to touch them. Some of the girls also touched her 'in another place'. Mary Warren warned her that if she spoke of this to anyone, she would be punished; at this point Mary Warren displayed a bone-handled kitchen knife. Emily Gehring stated that the girls met every night, at different times and places, in groups of five or six or seven; and she further stated that members of the group were continually changing and that she was told about other groups meeting in other places. The girls always removed their shirts, fondled and kissed each other, sometimes painted their breasts with snakes and strange symbols, and initiated others into their secret practices. Emily Gehring remembered, and listed, the names of sixteen girls. By the end of May, according to her statement, she could no longer live with herself, and two days later she delivered to the *Town Reporter* her written confession and urged the town authorities to stop the sisterhood, which was spreading among the girls of David Johnson Junior High like a disease.

The defence of Mary Warren

In response to these charges, which shocked our community, Mary Warren issued a detailed rebuttal that appeared in the *Town Reporter* on 4 June. She began by saying that absolute silence was the rule of the sisterhood and that any statement whatever about the group by one of its members was punished by instant expulsion. Nevertheless, the attack by Emily Gehring had convinced her that she must speak out in defence of the sisterhood even at the expense of banishment. She acknowledged that she had contacted Emily Gehring, who had been selected for initiation by a group of 'searchers' whom she refused to name; that she had passed Emily Gehring the blackened piece of paper and had met her, in the presence of two other members, whom she also refused to name, at the back of the Presbyterian Church at midnight and led her into the woods. From this point on, Mary Warren stated, Emily Gehring's report was utterly false, a vicious, hurtful attack the motive for which was all too clear. For Emily Gehring had failed to report that on 30 May she had been expelled from the sisterhood for *violating the vow of silence*. It is not clear from Mary Warren's defence precisely what the vow of silence demanded of a member or how Emily Gehring violated it, but it is clear, according to her statement, that Emily Gehring was deeply upset by the order of expulsion and threatened to take revenge. Mary Warren then repeated that Emily Gehring's confession was nothing but vicious lies and she stated that she refused, by reason of her vow, to discuss the sisterhood in any way, except to say that it was a noble, pure society dedicated to silence. She feared that the slander of Emily Gehring had caused harm and she ended with a passionate plea to the parents of our town to disregard the lies of Emily Gehring and trust their daughters.

Night worries

We were of two minds concerning Mary Warren's denial, for if on the one hand we were impressed by her intelligence and grateful to her for giving us grounds for doubting the confession of Emily Gehring, on the other hand her silence about the sisterhood raised doubts of a different kind and tended to undermine the case she was attempting to make. We noted with concern the existence of the group of 'searchers', the ritual of the blackened paper, the secret meeting in the woods, the rigorous vow; we wondered, if the girls were innocent, what it was they vowed not to reveal. It was at this time that we began to wake in the night and to ask ourselves how we had failed our daughters. Now reports first began to circulate of bands of girls roaming the night, crossing backyards, moving in the dark; and we began to hear rumours of strange cries, of painted breasts, of wild dances under the summer moon.

The death of Lavinia Hall

The daughters of our town, many of whom we suspected of being secret members of the sisterhood, now began to seem moody, restless and irritable. They refused to speak to us, shut themselves in their rooms, demanded that we leave them alone. These moody silences we took as proof of their membership; we hovered, we spied, we breathed down their necks. It was in this tense and oppressive atmosphere that on 12 June, ten days after the confession of Emily Gehring, fourteen-year-old Lavinia Hall climbed the two flights of stairs to the guest room in her parents' attic and there, lying down on a puffy comforter sewn by her grandmother, swallowed twenty of her father's sleeping pills. She left no note, but we knew that Lavinia Hall had been named by Emily Gehring as a member of the sisterhood and a participant in their erotic rites. Later it was learned from her parents that the Gehring confession had devastated Lavinia, a quiet, scholarly girl who practised Czerny exercises and Mozart sonatas on the piano two hours every day after school, kept a diary and stayed up late at night reading fantasy trilogies with twisting vines on the covers. After Emily Gehring's confession, Lavinia had refused to answer any questions about the sister-hood and had begun to act strangely, shutting herself up in her room for hours at a time and moving around the house restlessly at night. One night at two in the morning her parents heard footsteps in the attic above their bedroom. They climbed the creaking wooden stairs and found Lavinia sitting in her pale-blue pyjamas on the moon-striped floor in front of her old doll's house, which had been moved into the attic at the end of the sixth grade and still contained eight roomfuls of miniature furniture. Lavinia sat with her arms hugging her raised knees. Her feet were bare. She was strangely still. Her mother remem-bered one detail: the long forearm, revealed by the pulled-back pyjama sleeve. In the doll's house three little dolls, thick with dust, sat stiffly in the moonlit living-room: the child on the cobwebbed couch, the mother on the rocker, the father on the armchair with tiny lace doilies. The parents blamed them-selves for not recognizing the seriousness of their daughter's condition and they condemned the sisterhood as a band of murderers.

The second confession of Emily Gehring

Scarcely had we begun to suffer the news of the death of Lavinia Hall when Emily Gehring released to the *Town Reporter* a second confession, which angered us and filled us with confusion. For in it she repudiated her earlier confession and, siding with Mary Warren against herself, accused herself of having fabricated the first confession in a spirit of revenge for her expulsion from the sisterhood. Emily Gehring now confessed that on the night of 14 May she had been led into the woods by Mary Warren and two other girls, as she had truthfully reported on 2 June, but that 'nothing at all' had happened there. Of her initiation she said only that it 'consisted of silence'; for the next two weeks she had met nightly with small groups of the sisterhood, during which 'not a single word' was uttered by anyone and 'nothing at all' took place. On 30 May she was expelled from the sisterhood for violating her vow: she had spoken of the secret society to her friend Susannah Mason, who in turn had spoken to Bernice Thurman, not knowing that Bernice was a secret member of the sisterhood. Emily Gehring now claimed that she had regretted her false confession from the moment she had given it to the *Town Reporter*, but had been ashamed to admit that she had lied. The death of Lavinia Hall had shocked her into confessing the truth. She took upon herself the blame for Lavinia Hall's death, apologized to the grieving parents and spoke fervently of the sisterhood as a pure, noble association that had given meaning to her life; and she looked forward to the day when the glorious sisterhood would spread from town to town and take over the world.

Response to the second confession

As might be expected, the second confession thoroughly damaged the credibility of Emily Gehring as a witness, but our doubts, which at first were directed at the confession of 2 June, soon turned upon the second confession itself. We noted that Emily Gehring used the very words of Mary Warren to describe the sisterhood; and this coincidence led some of us to argue that Emily Gehring had been persuaded by Mary Warren to retract her confession and take upon herself all blame, in return for reinstatement in the sisterhood or for some other reward we could only guess at. Others noted with distaste the fervent turn at the end and argued that if Emily Gehring was now telling the truth, then the truth was both incomplete and disturbing. For if in fact the girls were innocent of the original charges, then the nature of the sisterhood remained carefully hidden, while at the same time its troubling power was revealed by the passion of an Emily Gehring, who couldn't tear herself away. In this view the second confession, while seeming to absolve the sisterhood, to reveal its innocence, in fact demonstrated an even more frightening truth about the secret society: its tenacious grip on the girls, the terrible loyalty it exacted from them.

The testimony of Dr Robert Meyer

It was during this time of uncertainty and anxiety that new information appeared from an unexpected quarter. Dr Robert Meyer, a dermatologist with an office on Broad Street, had been deeply disturbed when his daughter Hilda was named by Emily Gehring in her confession of 2 June. His daughter, he said, had called Emily Gehring a liar but had refused to speak of the sisterhood; after the first confession she became moody and irritable, and he could hear her pacing about at night. After three nights of terrible insomnia Robert Meyer made a fateful decision: he determined to follow his daughter and disrupt her sexual experiments. At midnight on the fourth night he heard her footsteps creaking in the hall. He threw off his covers, slipped into sweat-pants, sweat-shirt and running shoes, and followed her into the cool summer night. A block from the house she was met by two other girls, whom Meyer did not know. The three girls, wearing jeans, T-shirts and nylon windbreakers tied around their waists, set off for the woods at the north end of town. Meyer, a deeply moral man, felt immense distaste and self-disgust as he pursued the three girls through the night, ducking behind trees like a spy in a late-night movie and creeping through backyards past swing sets, badminton nets and fat plastic baseball bats. It struck him that he was doing something at once unsavoury and absurd. He did not know what he planned to do when he arrived at the woods, but of one thing he was certain: he would bring his daughter home. Once in the woods he was forced to advance with fanatical caution, since the snap of a single twig might give him away; he was reminded of boyhood walks on pine-needle trails, which became confused with childhood day-dreams about Indians in hushed forests. The girls crossed a stream and emerged in a small moonlit clearing well protected by pines. Four other girls were already present in the clearing. Standing behind a thick oak at a distance of some twenty feet from the group, Meyer experienced, in addition to his self-revulsion, an intense fear of what he was about to witness. The seven girls did not speak, although they greeted one another with nods. Following what appeared to be a prearranged plan, the girls formed a small, close circle and raised their arms in such a way that all their forearms crossed. After this silent sign the girls separated and took up isolated positions, sitting against separate trees or lying with arms clasped behind the head. Not a single word was uttered. Nothing happened. After thirty-five minutes by his watch, Meyer turned and crept away.

Response to Meyer's testimony

Meyer's testimony, far from resolving the problem of the sisterhood, plunged us into deeper controversy. Enemies of the sisterhood heaped scorn on Meyer's report, although they disagreed about the nature of its untrustworthiness. Some insisted that Meyer had invented the whole thing in a crude effort to protect his daughter; others argued that clever Hilda Meyer had plotted the entire episode, cunningly leading her father to the woods in order to have him witness a staged scene: The Innocent Maidens in Repose. Others pointed out that even if no deception had been practised, by either Robert Meyer or his daughter, the testimony was in no sense decisive: Meyer by his own admission did not remain during the entire meeting, he observed the girls only a single time and he observed only a single group of girls out of many groups. Was it not unlikely, people asked, was it not highly unlikely, that girls between the ages of twelve and fifteen would sneak out of their houses night after night, risking parental disapproval and even punishment, in order to meet with other girls in secluded and possibly dangerous places, solely for the purpose of doing nothing? This was not necessarily to say that the girls were engaging in forbidden deeds, although such deeds could never be ruled out, but merely to suggest that what they did do remained exasperatingly unknown. It was even possible that the girls, at the very time they were being observed by Meyer, had engaged in secret practices that he had failed to recognize; perhaps they had developed a system of signs and signals that Meyer had not been able to read.

The town

Night after night the members of the secret sisterhood set forth from their snug and restful rooms, the rooms of their child-hood, to seek out dark and hidden places. Sometimes we see, or think we see, a group of them vanishing into the shadows of backyards lit by kitchen windows, or gliding out of sight along a dark front lawn. Disdainful of our wishes, indifferent to our unhappiness, they seem a race apart, wild creatures of the night with streaming hair and eyes of fire, until we recall with a start that they are our daughters. What shall we do with our daughters? Uneasily we keep watch over them, fearful of provoking them to open defiance. Some say that we should lock our daughters in their rooms at night, that we should place bars on their windows, that we should punish them harshly, over and over again, until they bow their heads in obedience. One father is said to tie his thirteen-year-old daughter to her bed at night with clothes-line rope and to reward her cries with blows from a leather belt. Most deplore such measures but remain uncertain what to do. Meanwhile our daughters are restless, night after night bands of girls are seen disappearing into dark places beyond the reach of street lights. The sisterhood is growing. There are reports of girls moving across the parking lot behind the lumber yard, meeting in the small wood behind the high-school tennis courts, climbing from the cellars of half-built houses, emerging from the boat shed by South Pond. Always they move at night, as if searching for something, something they cannot find in sunlight; and we who remain at home, awake in the dark, seem to hear, like the distant hum of trucks on the throughway, a continual faint sound of footfalls moving lightly across dark lawns and dim-lit roads, over pebbled driveways and kerbside sand, through black leaves on forest paths, a ceaseless rustle of lines of footfalls weaving and unweaving in the night.

Explanations

Some say that the girls gather together in covens to practise the art of witchcraft under the guidance of older girls; there is talk of spells, potions, a goat-haired figure, wild seizures and abandons. Others say that the girls are a sisterhood of the moon: they dance to the ancient moon-goddess, dedicating themselves to her cold and passionate mysteries. Some say that the sisterhood, made restless by the boredom and emptiness of middle-class life, exists solely for the sake of erotic exploration. Others see in this explanation a desire to denigrate women, and insist that the sisterhood is an intellectual and political association dedicated to the ideal of freedom. Still others reject these explanations and argue that the sisterhood betrays all the marks of a religious cult: the initiation, the vow, the secret meetings, the fanatical loyalty, the refusal to break silence. The many explanations, far from casting rays of sharp and separate light on the hidden places of the sisterhood, have gradually interpenetrated and thickened to form a cloudy darkness, within which the girls move unseen.

The unknown

Like other concerned citizens, I have brooded nightly over the sisterhood and the proliferating explanations, until the darkness outside my window becomes streaked with grey. I have asked myself why we seem unable to pierce their secret, why we can't catch them in the act. If I believe that I have at last discovered the true explanation, the one we should have seen from the beginning, it isn't because I know something that others do not know. It's rather that my explanation honours the unknown and unseen, takes them into account as part of what is actually known. For it is precisely the element of the unknown, which looms so large in the case, that must be part of any solution. The girls, as we try to imagine them, keep vanishing into the unknown. They are penetrated by the unknown as by some black fluid. Is it possible that our search for the secret is misguided because we fail to include the unknown as a crucial element in that secret? Is it possible that our loathing of the unknown, our need to dispel it, to destroy it, to violate it through sharp, glittering acts of understanding, makes the unknown swell with dark power, as if it were some beast feeding on our swords? Are we perhaps searching for the wrong secret, the secret we ourselves long for? Or, to put it another way, is it possible that the secret lies open before us, that we already know what it is?

The secret of the sisterhood

I submit that we know everything that needs to be known in order to penetrate the mystery of the Sisterhood of Night. Dr Robert Meyer, sole witness to a gathering, reported that nothing whatever took place during the thirty-five minutes he observed the girls. In her second confession Emily Gehring insisted that nothing happened, that nothing ever happened, there in the dark. I suggest that these are scrupulously accurate descriptions. I submit that the girls band together at night not for the sake of some banal and titillating rite, some easily exposed hidden act, but solely for the sake of withdrawal and silence. The members of the sisterhood wish to be inaccessible. They wish to elude our gaze, to withdraw from investigation – they wish, above all, *not to be known*. In a world dense with understanding, oppressive with explanation and insight and love, the members of the silent sisterhood long to evade definition, to remain mysterious and ungraspable. Tell us! we cry, our voices shrill with love. Tell us everything! Then we will forgive you. But the girls do not wish to tell us anything, they don't wish to be heard at all. They wish, in effect, to become invisible. Precisely for this reason they cannot engage in any act that might reveal them. Hence their silence, their love of night solitude, their ritual celebration of the dark. They plunge into secrecy as into black smoke: in order to disappear.

In the night

I maintain that the Sisterhood of Night is an association of adolescent girls dedicated to the mysteries of solitude and silence. It is a high wall, a locked door, a face turning away. The sisterhood is a secret society that can never be disrupted, for even if we were to prevent the girls from meeting at night, even if we were to tie them to their beds for their entire lives, the dark purposes of the association would remain untouched. We cannot stop the sisterhood. Fearful of mystery, suspicious of silence, we accuse the members of dark crimes that secretly soothe us – for then, will we not know them? For we prefer witchcraft to silence, naked orgies to night stillness. But the girls long to be closed in silence, to become pale statues with blank eyes and breasts of stone. What shall we do with our daughters? Nightly the secret sisterhood moves through our town. There is talk of the sisterhood spreading to younger girls, to older girls; even the wives of our town seem to us restless, evasive. We long to confront our silent daughters with arguments, with violence;

we wake in the night from dreams of bleeding animals. Some say the sisterhood must be exposed and punished, for once such ideas take root, who will be able to stop them? Those of us who counsel patience are accused of cowardice. Already there is talk of bands of youths who roam the town at night armed with pointed sticks. What shall we do with our daughters? In the night we wake uneasily and tiptoe to their doors, pausing with our hands outstretched, unable to advance or retreat. We think of the long years of childhood, the party frocks and lollipops, the shimmer of trembling bubbles in blue summer air. We dream of better times.

The way out

1

Harter had expected the affair to end badly, but he hadn't
expected it to end as badly as it did: he on the edge of the bed,
grimly fastening the buttons of his shirt, she tearful and asprawl
in her lavender nightie, the one that made him long for
slimmer, younger, more desirable women, and then the surprise
he ought to have foreseen, the little twist of fate that turned it
all into farce – the suddenly opened door and the irate husband
striding into the room. So that's that, Harter thought, he's
going to kill me. But after a single step the husband stopped as if
struck in the face and Harter realized that only now had he
raised his eyes to the unpleasant scene before him. Harter
realized something else: he was going to get away with it. The
man by the door was small and neat, almost delicate, no match
for Harter. He wore a dark three-piece suit and a trim little
moustache, and his dark, thinning hair was combed back in
little waves over both temples. The exposed temples made him
look oddly frail, as if the blow of a fist would crush his skull like
a baby's and Harter felt a motion of pity for the little man, who

stood there without moving, without saying anything. Harter buttoned his shirt and stood up. He did not look at Martha. He walked slowly and carefully around the bed towards the door, and as he passed close to Martha's husband – was his name Joseph? Lawrence? – he saw that the man was not looking at him but staring straight ahead and that he was trembling. Harter was on the verge of saying something ridiculous – it's over anyway, none of it matters, she loves you – when the man spoke in a low, stifled voice, a voice so low that Harter could catch only the hiss of hate and something that sounded like 'you in the morning'. Harter passed quickly through the door and down the carpeted stairs to the living-room. In the light of the table lamp a slender black briefcase gleamed on the cushion of the armchair. Only as he stepped onto the front porch did Harter realize that the little man had been trembling with rage.

The moon startled him. It was disturbingly bright, like a white sun. It threw shadows of trees against the high stone wall of the park across the street and polished the fender of his car discreetly parked a block away. The night sky dark blue, a touch of autumn coldness in the air – a night for young lovers walking arm in arm, the sharp, exciting knock of high heels on sidewalks, muffled laughter, the scritch scritch of stockings on striding legs. He'd been a fool not to break it off sooner.

As Harter bent into his car he saw two library books on the passenger seat and remembered the third, lying on the night table by Martha's bed. She would have to return it for him. The thought of this future act of hers, which she would perform bravely, letting her hand linger as she placed the book on the return desk, gave him a strange sort of pleasure, as if he enjoyed being present in her life a little longer, as if it all weren't so depressingly final. Maybe he would see her again after a while. He would step up to her and place a hand on her shoulder. She would turn around, her eyes would fill with tears, or no, he would be reading in the library one night, he would look up and there, sitting across from him – but he was being sentimental. It was over and done with. Harter started towards the other side of town, where he lived alone on the top floor of a three-family house. Was it really one in the morning? The little man had no right bursting in like that. But then, it was his room and he hadn't really burst in, the door had opened rather slowly. He need never have known. Harter could have slipped out of her life as easily as you pulled off a sock at the end of the day, leaving it a bit wrinkled, a little the worse for wear, but no more. No, that had an ugly ring to it. He was tired, tired – tired of everything. And then, on the very night when he had finally found a way, the suddenly opened door, the little husband striding in. Now Harter had to carry away the image of the hissing little man, the shamed wife, the terrible scene he would never witness. And the worst part was, even though he had finally broken it off, even though he had grown sick to death of it all, the thought of Martha's tender reconciliation with her little husband did nothing to soothe his conscience. Instead it left him with a vague jealousy, as if he himself would have liked to be the one to wipe her tears away and forgive her for straying.

Harter was very tired, he scarcely noticed where he was driving, and he was startled to see his block suddenly before him. He had left the light on over the sink in the kitchen – the only yellow window on a dark, sleeping street. The little man had stopped suddenly, as if struck in the face. Harter closed the car door with care, disengaging the handle and nudging the door shut with his hip. He fumbled for his house key, wearily he climbed the stairs to the third floor, and that night he dreamed that he was playing the piano in the living-room of his childhood house. Martha was sitting close to him on the piano bench, a warm, drowsy feeling was filling him from the contact of her thigh, but when he turned to look at her he saw that the little husband was standing directly behind her, pressing his body against her back and twisting her ear in his little white fist.

2

Harter at thirty was a large soft man with broad round shoulders and a boyish face. He liked to wear single-colour dress shirts with the cuffs rolled back once, soft pre-washed Wrangler jeans and old loafers with thick socks. He taught history – ancient, modern and American – at a community college at the edge of a bad neighbourhood and played a lazy, good-natured game of tennis.

Although Harter had had his share of women, they always proved unsatisfactory, and unsatisfactory in the same way: finally, when all was said and done, they did not excite him enough, did not drive him to the pitch of frenzy he longed for. Sometimes he thought that the pattern of his erotic life had been set in the seventh grade, when for months he had desperately pursued a girl called Lois Bishop. At first she had ignored him cruelly, but his persistence, his devotion, perhaps even his suffering, had slowly made an impression, and one day she had consented to let him walk home with her – and it was during that walk, in the midst of an exhilaration so intense that it made his muscles feel sore, that he began to notice certain flaws in Lois Bishop which he hadn't noticed before, when she existed in the realm of the utterly inaccessible: a certain way the tip of her nose moved down and up when she talked, a certain harshness in her jaw, a disturbing boniness in her wrists and long thumbs. She seemed to like him, but he never asked to walk home with her again, and when he passed her in the halls he became cool and aloof. The same disappointment returned in high school, when in the act of sliding his hand to the top of Bernice Coleman's stocking on her living-room couch at eleven-thirty at night he suddenly imagined the beautiful, shimmering, unbearably desirable legs of Sharon Krupka, who sat across from him in the circle of maplewood desk-chairs in Problems of

American Democracy and who had a habit of crossing and uncrossing her legs over and over again, slowly, restlessly, tormentingly. In college, sophomore year, he had met a shy, not bad-looking girl, with eyeglasses and a self-deprecating sense of humour, who had surprised him into bed with her one afternoon, while all along he could think only of her roommate, a brassy blonde who liked to wear black tights and leather miniskirts, believed in astrology and Scientology, and had a way of sitting on chairs with her legs thrown carelessly over the arms. His handful of adult affairs had all suffered from the same theme of disappointment: the thin, quiet, older woman he had met at a party, who had seemed so relieved at finding someone to talk to and who had proved on better acquaintance to have a flood of bitter grievances against her mother, her boss, the horrible men in her life and finally against Harter himself; the heavyish psychology teacher who used too much perfume and required continual, exhausting assurances that he found her attractive; the fairly pretty artist he had met at another party, who laughed explosively, throwing back her head, but who in bed became silent and melancholy, as if locked in a secret sorrow. There had been others, all of whom had seemed promising but had quickly revealed a crucial flaw. And always behind or above these women was some other, fatally desirable woman, whom he longed for but could never possess – someone glimpsed on a bus, or on a beach, or on some glossy poster advertising liquor – women who haunted his imagination and followed him into bed, where they mocked the mediocre actual woman who had already become unsatisfactory.

Although Harter felt he should have slept with many more women, and was troubled by a shyness he seemed unable to overcome, he knew that women liked him well enough. He was a sympathetic listener and his sympathy had a way of leading sooner or later to physical intimacy, but sometimes he wondered whether he deliberately sought out troubled women so that he could gain their affection without much effort – after which it was never long before their rather obvious flaws proved fatal. In darker moods he wondered whether he was cursed with a romantic temperament. Harter liked to call himself a romantic, especially in conversation with women, by which he implied that he was a mysterious man full of endless enthusiasms and passions, but by which he in fact meant that nothing, especially a woman, could satisfy him for long. Why are we born? Where are we going? These were some of the questions that Harter liked to put to himself, from time to time, when the hours grew heavy on his hands; and for this reason he was fond of calling himself a philosopher.

He had met Martha in the reading room of the city library, where he liked to go several evenings a week to leaf through current magazines and look at the high-school girls, wondering which of them would turn up in his classes in a year or two. The bodies of teenage girls excited him, though he was far too timid ever to start anything with one of them; but there was no harm in looking. He liked to pick out girls of special grace and elegance, with their cornsilk hair, white blouses and knee-length kilts, but he also liked tough working-class girls with rouged cheeks, shiny black leather jackets, bright red nails and jeans so tight they looked painful.

One rainy evening shortly before closing time he checked out a book and stepped with his umbrella through the door of the main room into the little lobby before the big glass front doors, where he saw a woman in a dark blue coat holding two books and looking out through the dripping glass with a worried expression. He had seen her once or twice before, reading a magazine or looking for a book. He joked about the rain and discovered she had parked two blocks away. She first refused and then accepted his offer to share his umbrella, and he led her carefully to her car, biting down his irritation when he stepped in a puddle up to his ankle and thinking how it was just his luck: not the two girls he had seen in the stacks that night, giggling over a big book in the art section, but this plumpish woman with her marriage ring. She thanked him earnestly. A week later he saw her again in the library, and this time she smiled and thanked him again. When he saw her two nights later they fell into conversation. She liked to read; her husband travelled a lot; she was always forgetting things like umbrellas. The next time he saw her they spoke easily, as if they were old friends, and one night she invited him to her home for a cup of tea.

At first the affair excited him – she was his first married woman – and he was grateful for the way she doted on him, spoiled him, listened to him with earnest attention. For whole minutes, as she stared at him, she would forget to blink her wide, generous eyes. It may have been the very completeness of her surrender that began to make him uneasy, but he soon grew dissatisfied and within a month he knew that he had made a mistake. He was not the adulterous type; at forty-three she was too old for him; the softness and ampleness of her flesh disturbed him. He began looking for a way to break it off cleanly, a way that would make it clear she was not to blame. He reminded himself that however much it might hurt her now, it would hurt her even more if he waited. He was certain he could find the right words. It was the best thing for all concerned.

3

Harter was awakened by a soft, persistent rapping on his door, such as someone might make who knew that it was early in the morning – not yet seven o'clock – and who wished to apologize for disturbing him even while insisting that he must be disturbed. Harter threw on an old robe and raked his fingers through his hair. He had not slept well. When he opened the kitchen door he was surprised to see two men in formal overcoats who stood with their hats in their hands. 'May we come in?' asked the older and taller man, whose thick grey hair was brushed carefully back above his ears, and when Harter hesitated the other said, 'We're here about – that business of last night. He asked us to speak to you.' He lowered his eyes. 'We can come back another time.'

'No, it's all right, I'm – it's not even seven. Come in.' Harter gave a little flourish with his hand, which at once he regretted for its air of frivolity, and stopping the gesture abruptly he thrust the hand into the slightly torn pocket of his robe.

The men took two steps into the small kitchen and stopped, gripping their homburgs. Harter began to pull a chair out from the table, noticing with distaste the coffee cup with its sticky brown sediment, the plate with its stale half-doughnut, the crusted spoon in the flowered sugar bowl. The men did not move towards the table and Harter, uncertain, stood with a hand resting on the chairback.

'Mr Harter,' said the older man, 'we regret the inconvenience and can only stay a few minutes ourselves. Our friend was particularly anxious for us to see you. Needless to say he's upset – very upset. He would like to meet with you as soon as possible.'

Harter imagined the meeting with revulsion and wondered whether there was some way he could get out of it. But the thought of avoiding the little man made him uncomfortable, as if he would be running away.

'I'll meet with him, why not, if he wants to. But what does he want?'

The second man said, 'Mr Harter, you don't have to meet with him if you don't want to. You have the right to refuse.'

'Although I wouldn't,' the older man said, 'if I were you.'

'Is that a threat?' Harter said angrily; and a little burst of fear rippled across his stomach.

The older man looked at him in surprise. 'Hardly. I regret the misunderstanding. I meant only that if you refuse to see him now, you'll have to see him later. He's very stubborn, our friend. And so it seems advisable not to draw things out, causing even more trouble and grief. But you do what you want to, of course.'

'Right,' said Harter. 'And I said I'd see him. Whenever.'

'Well, good. That makes our job that much easier. Would tomorrow suit you? In the morning: early. We both work.'

Harter hesitated. 'I'm not really at my best, early in the morning.'

The older man glanced down at his hat and raised his eyes. 'Mr Harter, may I say something? You have been the cause, for reasons of your own, of great pain and suffering. Do you seriously mean that for the sake of a few hours' sleep you would refuse to meet with the injured party at a time convenient for him?'

Harter felt a motion of anger and tightened his grip on the chair. He ought to throw the old bastard out on his ear. But the man's tone had not been insolent and his face revealed only a mild surprise.

Harter shrugged. 'Whenever. Where does he –'

'Oh, don't worry,' said the other, 'we'll be getting back to you.'

'But why?' Harter began and decided to drop it.

'Fine,' said the older man, putting his hat on his head. 'Then it's agreed. We can go now.'

The other man stepped forward. 'If you should change your mind –'

'We needn't consider that,' said the man wearing the hat,

who had already stepped over to the door and stood with his hand on the fluted glass knob.

'I told you I'd meet with him,' Harter said, in a voice that struck him as a little too loud, even shrill, and he made an effort to master himself. 'Listen, I hardly slept at all last night.'

The two men exchanged glances and said nothing.

'Until later, then,' said the man in the hat, moving through the doorway onto the landing. The second man followed, holding his hat in one hand and closing the door quietly with the other. Through the brass window grille, half covered by frilly white curtains, Harter could see the backs of their heads, moving away.

Harter spent the next hour failing to fall asleep, and after a long shower and two cups of coffee he drove out of town into the country. The sugar maples had started to turn; on the far hills they looked like coloured gumdrops. A small white sign pointed him onto a familiar dirt road overhung with branches and he soon came to an old red barn filled with books. The bulb-lit dark aisles smelled of damp wood. Harter liked to read about the Revolutionary War – from time to time he thought of writing a longish essay on the effects of the muzzle-loading musket on campaign strategy, but nothing had ever come of it – and he was looking through a monograph on the Danbury campaign when out of the corner of his eye he saw Martha in her blue coat at the end of the aisle. Even as he drew in his breath sharply he realized his mistake: she was older than Martha, heavier, hardly like her at all. He had sucked in his breath – an unmistakable gasp. Harter thrust the booklet back on the shelf and strode through the bulb-lit barn into the bright day.

The barn was red, the sky was blue. Along one side of the building was a row of bookstalls stuffed with paperbacks and sliced into sun and shade. A girl of about eighteen stood bent over a shady stall and as she moved partway into brilliant sunlight, something flashed for an instant: a tiny ear-ring? She had very short straw-coloured hair parted on one side, and she wore crisp-looking dark blue jeans with the cuffs rolled up above the calf and a long-sleeved white shirt that came down over her buttocks. The flash reminded Harter of something, it was on the tip of his mind, but at the sound of his footsteps on the gravel the girl glanced up and let her gaze linger for a moment before she returned to browsing. And Harter was seized by the certainty that she was approachable, that he could strike up a conversation with her, maybe even drive off with her to a country inn for a cup of coffee: she had let her gaze linger that extra moment. He would tell her everything. She would be moved by his unhappiness, she would reach across the table and place her hand on the back of his hand – and as Harter turned back to his car, for it was all impossible and absurd, he imagined that in the space of that arrested glance she had seen, in the grave face of a stranger, a secret grief.

At home Harter lay down heavily on his bed, but even as he closed his eyes he could feel his heart beating with disturbing swiftness. He could almost feel the blood surging through his veins as it rushed to reach the farthest limits of his body: his toes, his fingertips, his tingling scalp. The little man had stopped suddenly, as if struck in the face. And Martha asprawl in her lavender nightie, blowing her nose into a pink tissue – he'd forgotten the pink tissue. The room had been nearly dark. Martha disliked the lamp on the night table, with its bright, revealing bulb, and on the first night she had insisted on dragging out some sort of glass lantern with thick red-and-blue panes. It was there on all his visits, to cast its dim, romantic light over the room and permit her to overcome, a little, the extreme modesty that at first he'd found so touching but that had come to irritate him more and more. The little man had entered quietly – Harter couldn't remember hearing the door-knob turn – and had taken a full step into the room before suddenly coming to a halt. He hadn't said anything but had stood rigidly there while Harter fumbled with his exasperating buttons. And now he remembered how Martha, with wisps of hair sticking to her wet cheeks, had pulled her nightie over her breasts, as if she were suddenly shy – a big, bewildered girl. For a few moments she stopped crying and stared at the man in the doorway, who did not move. Harter wished he had paid more attention to the few things she'd ever said about him, but the truth was, he hadn't wanted to think about the husband at all. He had made it abundantly clear to Martha that he wished to be spared the details of her married life. Although Martha had an annoying habit of refusing to speak unkindly of people, she had once called her husband 'stubborn'; Harter hadn't invited her to give instances. Another time she had called him 'old-fashioned', which somehow made Harter imagine that he wore well-polished shoes with little holes in the toes and liked his socks to be rolled into balls. He had never asked a single question about the man, whose photograph he had seen only once on the bureau before Martha had made a habit of concealing it. His last name was odd: Razumian. He travelled a lot. A salesman, was he? A stubborn and old-fashioned little man. He wanted to meet with Harter. But why? Maybe he needed assurances. Harter was in no mood to rehash the sorry affair, but he supposed he'd have to go through with it. Your wife loves you. She's lonely, that's all. We just happened to meet – just one of those things. It's over. Nothing serious. He had hissed out some words.

Harter opened his eyes and saw by the yellow light coming through the window that it was late afternoon. He had fallen asleep for nearly two hours. His night's sleep was now in jeopardy – and the men were coming back early in the morning. How could he possibly have allowed himself to be manipulated into such a foolish promise? His head felt tight, as if at any second it would burst into the full flower of headache, and suddenly a ripple of nervousness passed across his stomach.

Harter sat up angrily. He had nothing to fear from the rigid little man and his peculiar friends. They would meet, and have it out, and that would be that. One meeting – no more. Harter swung his legs decisively over the side of the bed, and as his feet struck the floor he remembered the girl stepping from shade partway into brilliant sunlight. Something flashed for an instant: a tiny ear-ring? It had reminded him of something else and he had it now, he had it: it was the clasp of the slender black briefcase, gleaming in the light of the living-room lamp.

Wearily Harter dragged himself into the kitchen to begin the long night.

4

Harter was walking along the narrow aisle of a library, following a girl who ran her fingers along the book spines. As he drew close to her she turned around, and he saw that she was a little girl in a short nightgown, with one bare shoulder and a Band-Aid on her knee. She wore bright red lipstick and smiled up at him, and as Harter bent over to kiss her shoulder she began to frown and suddenly seized his upper arm and squeezed painfully, saying, 'Get up! Get! Up get!' Harter opened his eyes. A voice in the dark said, 'Get up.' He sat up violently, sick with fear, but already he understood, he knew exactly what was happening.

'How did you get in here?' he said, making a fist. 'There are laws, I can call the police.'

'The police!' said the voice of the older man. 'But there's no need to do that, now is there, Mr Harter? We told you we'd be back. And you ought to take a minute to consider whether you really want anyone to know why we're here. Of course, we regret waking you like this, at such an early hour. But you were so fast asleep! I'm afraid you left us no choice. You have my word we knocked.'

'Yes, we knocked, you can rest easy on that. We each knocked twice.'

'And the door was unlocked, Mr Harter, as if you'd left it that way on purpose. "He must have left it like that on purpose," my friend said. "For us." But you've got to get up now, there's no time to waste.'

'It's the middle of the night,' Harter said, but even as he spoke he bent towards his clock and saw that it was nearly five. 'Not that I can sleep anyway. A terrible night.' And flinging the covers off he swung his legs so forcefully over the side of the bed that one of the men leaped back.

'But you agreed to meet,' said the older man, who had remained near the bed. 'That was understood. We thought everything had been arranged.'

'All this is wrong,' Harter said, stepping out of bed towards the chair, where he had laid his shirt and pants.

'I think we can all agree that it's *wrong*, Mr Harter. The question is, how to bring about a satisfactory resolution to the problem. As to the early hour, certainly we apologize, though in all fairness you have to admit that we too are up very early, on business that doesn't directly concern us. We'd be very grateful if you hurried, we have to go to work ourselves – a full day's work, after only five hours of sleep. Do you have any idea what it's like to work a full day after only five hours of sleep? But this isn't an ordinary day, as I'm sure you'll agree.'

'Not an ordinary day at all,' said the other. 'At least, not in the ordinary sense.'

'But why are we talking so much?' Harter said, snatching up his clothes and turning towards the bathroom. 'I'd like to get this over with as much as he does.' In the bathroom he rubbed water on his face and fumbled into his clothes – he felt as if he were wearing gloves, he could barely thrust the slippery buttons through the tiny shirt holes – and as he ran a comb through his hair in the dimness of the night-light it struck him that all this was absurd, he ought to throw them out and go back to sleep and deal with it all in the clear light of morning. It seemed to him that at the slightest show of resistance they would back down and leave him alone, he even wondered whether they were secretly hoping for him to let them off the hook – after all, hadn't one of the men hinted from the very beginning that they found the whole business as distasteful as he did? But he was impatient himself to get it over with. If the little man was itching to see him, then he for one wasn't going to be difficult; and as he reached out to wipe his fingers on a towel, he jerked his hands away as a dark moth burst silently from the folds.

With a finger raised to his lips he began to lead them down the shadowy stairway, lit at each landing by a twenty-five-watt bulb in a yellow oilpaper shade with brown scorch marks.

On the dark front porch he could see the plumes of his breath. The sight of his feathery frail-looking breath made him feel cold and a little strange, as if someone his size ought to have breath more solid than that. The sky was blackish grey, tinged at the horizon with a sulphurous glow. No stars: only that glow staining the sky from neon signs and sodium-vapour lamps. The tops of gabled two-family houses showed black against the sky.

The men led him towards a parked car. 'Where are we going?' Harter whispered as he slid into the front seat.

'To your meeting,' the older man said. Harter felt a deep desire to close his eyes. His lids burned, he felt warm, feverish, and he remembered how, as a child, on late-night car trips, he had struggled to keep awake as he swooned in and out of half-sleep, surrendering more and more to the soothing weariness that spread in him like a sweetness. Suddenly he sat up stiffly. It was important to remain alert. The car had left his street and was passing Koslowski's grocery, where in the greenish light of a street lamp a rust-coloured cat sat on top of a garbage can with his paws tucked under his chest. In the dark glass of the store window Harter could see a telephone pole and, through the pole, a dim pyramid of soup cans. He closed his eyes for a moment and when he opened them he saw gas stations and body shops slipping by. Dark trucks moved on the street, big eighteen-wheelers heading for the throughway. Two raspberry-red gas pumps glowed under whitish lights and in a brilliant yellow diner a man in a zippered jacket bent over a cup. A truck door slammed. Then they were floating up an entrance ramp and from the throughway Harter looked down at green or orange street lamps in curving rows, dark factories with broken windows, oil drums shaped like immense tins of shoe polish against a murky band of sky. 'Where did you say we,' Harter heard himself saying, and he thought he heard the word 'rendezvous', which began to hum in his mind, ronday vooronday vooronday, and vaguely he wondered where all the old street lamps had gone to, the comforting old street lamps that seemed to cast a kinder light. Then he was bumping along a badly paved road between fields of high grass and stretches of unpainted fence. They came to a stop on a slope of grass before a wood. Harter could feel the car tilted a little to one side. The trees were black against the paling sky. Another car was parked ten feet away.

They're going to murder me, Harter thought and when he got out of the car he stopped after taking a single step. 'I don't know what you're up to,' he said, 'but I'm not going in there.'

The men looked at each other and looked away.

'Of course,' the older man said with sudden weariness, 'it's entirely up to you.' He lowered his voice. 'I shouldn't say this, but I admit I don't much care for this way of handling matters.' He raised his voice slightly. 'I think I should add you've nothing to fear from us. We're not your friends, Mr Harter – far from it. We're his friends, and we don't care at all for the way you've behaved towards him. But it would be a mistake to assume that we're your enemies, even though we've brought you here at his request. We can't force you to this meeting – wouldn't if we could. It's up to you entirely. Of course, you'll hear from him again. He's not the sort of man to let things drop, especially in a painful business of this kind. He'll insist on meeting with you. He'll never give up. Sooner or later –'

'Oh, let's get on with it!' said Harter, for the entire adventure had suddenly assumed a grotesque air. The two men, the dawn reckoning, the gloomy wood – actually Lincoln Forest, where he had picnicked only the week before – it was all the stuff of old movies whose titles you could never remember. He had injured the little man, and so he had to get up in the middle of the night and go through the motions of a farcical encounter of some kind. That much seemed clear. The two men looked at each other, appeared to hesitate and turned towards the path. Hurter followed, with a glance at the other car – Martha's car? He was sure of it. Of course: the little man's car. For an instant he imagined Martha tied up inside, with a gag in her mouth, struggling, twisting, but he shook his head sharply and followed the men onto the path.

Dawn was rising, overhead the sky was dark grey with a whitish streak, but night still clung to the forest path. They walked single file: first the older man, then Harter, then the second man. A pungent forest smell made Harter's eyes sting, a smell of moist earth, sweet rotting wood and lush ferns the size of peacock feathers. And an odd exhilaration seized him, as he sucked in the sharp fresh air, which made the tissues in his nose tingle and brought water to his eyes. He was going to make amends. He would give the little man all the assurance he needed – and wasn't the very fact of his presence here proof of his goodwill? He had never intended any harm. Harter's senses felt wide open, he seemed to take everything in: the great rubbery white growths on a trunk, like saucers stuck in the tree, the yellow gum wrapper lying against a root, the pale, pale blue piece of sky between black leaves, the chuk-chuk-chuk of some bird, like the sound of a spoon rapping the rim of a wooden salad bowl.

The path turned and seemed to become less dark. What was happening? Orange mushrooms grew on top of a rotting stump, overhead the sky was grey-white and pale blue, and it seemed to Harter that a darkness was lifting from inside him, too. He had done a bad thing. He had never meant to hurt anyone, but he'd done it anyway. He had hurt Martha and then the little husband, and now he would make amends. It seemed to Harter that if only he could find the right words, he might be the instrument of their reconciliation, and even of a new and deeper life between them. A new life! Yes, and what of his own life? What about that? He breathed deep, taking in the pungent earthy-green smell. He'd allowed himself to fall into shabbiness. He would change all that. He had become stuck in his life and now he saw a way out. It was all connected somehow with the sharp-smelling air, and the strange orange mushrooms, and the brightening sky; and he felt a warm, melting friendliness for these men who had shaken him out of his torpor and were leading him towards a revelation they couldn't be expected to understand. The world was opening up, bursting with details he had never bothered to notice. He would pay attention to things. He would change his life. And at the thought of the immensity of what he had to say, a doubt came over him and a funny feeling rippled across his stomach. I've got to get a grip on myself, thought Harter, and as the path began to climb he sucked in sharp, deep draughts of air.

'This way. Over here,' said the leader, and Harter followed him off the path and through a space of trees with nearly smooth places between them. Harter saw everything very sharply. It all seemed to have a meaning for him, a meaning that had always been there but that he had failed to understand, as if he had spent his life with his head turned in the wrong direction. Suddenly he stepped into a clearing. Morning light lay on a broad sweep of cuff-high grass. The tops of the highest trees were in sunlight. In the darkness at one end of the clearing stood the little man, stiff and unmoving. He wore a dark suit and held a trench coat over one arm.

The two men walked over to him. A yellow butterfly rose from the grass and Harter watched its crazed, nervous flight in astonishment.

The two men walked to the middle of the clearing and spoke for a moment before the older man walked slowly and deliberately away from the other. No one seemed to be paying attention to Harter, who felt a sudden shyness, as if he were a schoolboy waiting to be noticed by the principal in his leathery brown office. The older man had stopped and was digging in the grass with his heel. Harter could feel a morning warmth beginning to penetrate the chill. It was going to be a hot, sunny autumn day.

The older man was now coming towards Harter, who looked up in surprise, as if he had forgotten where he was. In the shade the little husband stood motionless, staring straight ahead. And it seemed to Harter that never, never would he be able to speak to this man, locked away in his stiff white anger. Harter felt how nice it would be to lie down in the soft grass for a moment and close his eyes; and a nervousness came over him, as he tried to remember what it was he had wanted to say.

'. . . at this mark,' said the man, who had led Harter across the grass and was pointing to the ground. Harter noticed that the man was placing something in his hand and he was surprised at how heavy it was, for an object so small. Bang bang you're dead. Somewhere in the woods a bird was banging a spoon against a wooden bowl, and suddenly Harter remembered his father striding into the room with a new comic book as he lay in bed with the mumps beside the open window. Through the window screen he could look down at the backyard swing with its two dirt patches, at the two crab-apple trees, at the garden with its rows of corn and its tall sticks for tomatoes, and on top of one of the sticks sat a bird that suddenly rose into the air and flew higher and higher into the blue sky. Harter looked down at the gun in his hand. He was standing in a field with a gun in his hand and it was all absurd, so absurd that he wanted to laugh out loud, but the thought of his loud laughter ringing through the quiet clearing made him uneasy and he reminded himself to pay close attention to what was happening. The man had explained something to him and was walking away, and now from the shade emerged the little husband in his dark suit and without his coat – where was his coat? – and strode into the field in the pale morning light, and stopped. In the light his face was very pale. The exposed temples seemed fragile as eggshell. Harter tried to remember what he had wanted to tell him back on the path, long ago, but he felt exhausted, his chest heaved and he stared with fascination at the pale little man across from him who stood at attention with his arm pressed to his side. Harter had the sensation that if he stepped up to the man and tapped him on the temple with a forefinger he would fall over in the grass. All at once Harter understood very clearly what was happening and he wondered whether he should shout or run away, but a giddiness seized him and he imagined himself bursting into loud, hysterical laughter – in another second they would all burst into laughter and big, fat tears would roll down their cheeks. One of the men was saying something to him and with a quick shake of his head Harter said 'No' and threw the gun away. He watched it move through the air and sink into high grass. He took a step forward and saw the little man raise his stiff arm. The arm reminded him of something, he had seen it long ago, back in his childhood, or maybe some other time, yes, now he had it: it was the arm of the cowboy in the penny arcade. But how long ago was long ago? Harter heard a sound like a shot. 'That's all over,' Harter said aloud and took another step before the ground slipped away from him. He had a fierce desire to explain something, something of immense importance, but it was difficult to collect his thoughts because his chest itched, somewhere a train was roaring, hundreds of yellow butterflies were beating their wings like mad.

Flying carpets

In the long summers of my childhood, games flared up suddenly, burned to a brightness and vanished forever. The summers were so long that they gradually grew longer than the whole year, they stretched out slowly beyond the edges of our lives, but at every moment of their vastness they were drawing to an end, for that's what summers mostly did: they taunted us with endings, marched always into the long shadow thrown backwards by the end of vacation. And because our summers were always ending, and because they lasted forever, we grew impatient with our games, we sought new and more intense ones; and as the crickets of August grew louder and a single red leaf appeared on branches green with summer, we threw ourselves as if desperately into new adventures, while the long days, never changing, grew heavy with boredom and longing.

I first saw the carpets in the backyards of other neighbourhoods. Glimpses of them came to me from behind garages, flickers of colour at the corners of two-family houses where clothes-lines on pulleys stretched from upper porches to high grey poles, and old Italian men in straw hats stood hoeing between rows of tomatoes and waist-high corn. I saw one once at the far end of a narrow strip of grass between two stucco houses, skimming lightly over the ground at the level of the garbage cans. Although I took note of them, they were of no more interest to me than games of jump rope I idly watched on the school playground, or dangerous games with jack-knives I saw the older boys playing at the back of the candy store. One morning I noticed one in a backyard in my neighbourhood; four boys stood tensely watching. I was not surprised a few days later when my father came home from work with a long package under his arm, wrapped in heavy brown paper, tied with straw-coloured twine from which little prickly hairs stuck up.

The colours were duller than I had expected, less magical – only maroon and green: dark green curlings and loopings against a maroon that was nearly brown. At each end the fringes were thickish rough strings. I had imagined crimson, emerald, the orange of exotic birds. The underside of the carpet was covered with a coarse, scratchy material like burlap; in one corner I noticed a small black mark, circled in red, shaped like a capital H with a slanting middle line. In the backyard I practised cautiously, close to the ground, following the blurred blue directions printed on a piece of paper so thin I could see my fingertips touching the other side. It was all a matter of artfully shifted weight: seated cross-legged just behind the centre of the carpet, you leaned forward slightly to send the carpet forward, left to make it turn left; right, right. The carpet rose when you lifted both sides with fingers cupped beneath, lowered when you pushed lightly down. It slowed to a stop when the bottom felt the pressure of a surface.

At night I kept it rolled up in the narrow space at the foot of my bed, alongside old puzzle boxes at the bottom of my bookcase.

For days I was content to practise gliding back and forth about the yard, passing under the branches of the crab-apple trees, squeezing between the swing and ladder of the yellow swing set, flying into the bottoms of sheets on the clothes-line, drifting above the row of zinnias at the edge of the garden to skim along the carrots and radishes and four rows of corn, passing back and forth over the wooden floor of the old chicken coop that was nothing but a roof and posts at the back of the garage, while my mother watched anxiously from the kitchen window. I was no more tempted to rise into the sky than I was tempted to plunge downhill on my bike with my arms crossed over my chest. Sometimes I liked to watch the shadow of my carpet moving on the ground, a little below me and to one side; and now and then, in a nearby yard, I would see an older boy rise on his carpet above a kitchen window, or pass over the sunlit shingles of a garage roof.

Sometimes my friend Joey came skimming over his low picket fence into my yard. Then I followed him around and around the crab-apple trees and through the open chicken coop. He went faster than I did, leaning far forward, tipping sharply left or right. He even swooped over my head, so that for a moment a shadow passed over me. One day he landed on the flat tar-papered roof of the chicken coop, where I soon joined him. Standing with my hands on my hips, the sun burning down on my face, I could see over the tall backyard hedge into the weed-grown lot where in past summers I had hunted for frogs and garden snakes. Beyond the lot I saw houses and telephone wires rising on the hill beside the curving sun-sparkling road; and here and there, in backyards hung with clothes-lines, against the white-shingled backs of houses, over porch rails and sloping cellar doors and the water-arcs of lawn sprinklers shot through with faint rainbows, I could see the children on their red and green and blue carpets, riding through the sunny air.

One afternoon when my father was at work and my mother lay in her darkened bedroom, breathing damply with asthma, I pulled out the carpet at the foot of the bed, unrolled it and sat down on it to wait. I wasn't supposed to ride my carpet unless my mother was watching from the kitchen window. Joey was in another town, visiting his cousin Marilyn, who lived near a department store with an escalator. The thought of riding up one escalator and down the next, up one and down the next, while the stairs flattened out or lifted up, filled me with irritation and boredom. Through the window screen I could hear the sharp, clear blows of a hammer, like the ticking of a gigantic clock. I could hear the clish-clish of hedge clippers, which made me think of movie sword fights; the uneven hum of a rising and falling bee. I lifted the edges of the carpet and began to float about the room. After a while I passed through the door and down the stairs into the small living-room and big yellow kitchen, but I kept bumping into pots and chair-tops; and soon I came skimming up the stairs and landed on my bed and looked out the window into the backyard. The shadow of the swing frame showed sharp and black against the grass. I felt a tingling or tugging in my legs and arms. Dreamily I pushed the window higher and raised the screen.

For a while I glided about the room, then bent low as I approached the open window and began to squeeze the carpet through. The wooden bottom of the raised window scraped along my back, the sides of the frame pressed against me. It was like the dream where I tried to push myself through the small doorway, tried and tried, though my bones hurt and my skin burned, till suddenly I pulled free. For a moment I seemed to sit suspended in the air beyond my window; below I saw the green hose looped on its hook, the handles and the handle-shadows on the tops of the metal garbage cans, the mountain laurel bush pressed against the cellar window; then I was floating out over the top of the swing and the crab-apple trees; below me I saw the shadow of the carpet rippling over grass; and drifting high over the hedge and out over the vacant lot, I looked down on the sunny tall grass, the milkweed pods and pink thistles, a green Coke bottle gleaming in the sun; beyond the lot the houses rose behind each other on the hill, the red chimneys clear against the blue sky; and all was sunny, all was peaceful and still; the hum of insects; the far sound of a hand mower, like distant scissors; soft shouts of children in the warm, drowsy air; heavily my eyelids began to close; but far below I saw a boy in brown shorts looking up at me, shading his eyes; and seeing him there, I felt suddenly where I was, way up in the dangerous air; and leaning fearfully to one side I steered the carpet back to my yard, dropped past the swing and landed on the grass near the back steps. As I sat safe in my yard I glanced up at the high, open window; and far above the window the red shingles of the roof glittered in the sun.

I dragged the heavy carpet up to my room, but the next day I rose high above Joey as he passed over the top of the swing. In a distant yard I saw someone skim over the top of a garage roof and sink out of sight. At night I lay awake planning voyages, pressing both hands against my heart to slow its violent beating.

One night I woke to a racket of crickets. Through the window screen I could see the shadow of the swing frame in the moonlit backyard. I could see the street lamp across from the bakery down by the field and the three street lamps rising with the road as it curved out of sight at the top of the hill. The night sky was the colour of a dark blue marble I liked to hold up to a bulb in the table lamp. I dressed quickly, pulled out my carpet and slowly, so as not to make scraping noises, pushed up the window and the screen. From the foot of the bed I lifted the rolled rug. It suddenly spilled open, like a dark liquid rushing from a bottle. The wood of the window pressed against my back as I bent my way through.

In the blue night I sailed over the backyard, passing high over the hedge and into the lot, where I saw the shadow of the carpet rippling over moonlit high grass. I turned back to the yard, swooped over the garage roof and circled the house at the level

of the upper windows, watching myself pass in the glittery black
glass; and rising a little higher, into the dark and dream-blue air,
I looked down to see that I was passing over Joey's yard towards
Ciccarelli's lot, where older boys had rock fights in the choked
paths twisting among high weeds and thornbushes; and as
when, standing up to my waist in water, I suddenly bent my
legs and felt the cold wetness covering my shoulders, so now I
plunged into the dark blue night, crossing Ciccarelli's lot,
passing over a street, sailing over garage roofs, till rising higher I
looked down on telephone wires glistening as if wet with
moonlight, on moon-greened tree-tops stuffed with blackness,
on the slanting rafters and open spaces of a half-built house
criss-crossed with shadows; in the distance I could see a glassy
stream going under a road; spots of light showed the shapes of
far streets; and passing over a roof close by a chimney, I saw
each brick so sharp and clear in the moonlight that I could
make out small bumps and holes in the red and ochre surfaces;
and sweeping upwards with the wind in my hair I flew over
moon-flooded rooftops striped with chimney shadows, until I
saw below me the steeple of a white church, the top of the
firehouse, the big red letters of the five-and-dime, the movie
marquee sticking out like a drawer, the shop windows dark-
shining in the light of street lamps, the street with its sheen of
red from the traffic light; then out over rows of rooftops on the
far side of town, a black factory with lit-up windows and white
smoke that glowed like light; a field stretching away; gleaming
water; till I felt I'd strayed to the farthest edge of things; and
turning back I flew high above the moonlit town, when
suddenly I saw the hill with three street lamps, the bakery, the
swing frame, the chicken coop – and landing for a moment on
the roof of the garage, sitting with my legs astride the peak,
exultant, unafraid, I saw, high in the blue night sky, passing
slowly across the white moon, another carpet with its rider.

With a feeling of exhilaration and weariness – a weariness like sadness – I rose slowly towards my window, and bending my way through, I plunged into sleep.

The next morning I woke sluggish and heavy-headed. Outside, Joey was waiting for me on his carpet. He wanted to race around the house. But I had no heart for carpets that day, stubbornly I swung on the old swing, threw a tennis ball onto the garage roof and caught it as it came rushing over the edge, squeezed through the hedge into the vacant lot where I'd once caught a frog in a jar. At night I lay remembering my journey in sharp detail – the moon-glistening telephone wires above their shadow-stripes, the clear bricks in the chimney – while through the window screen I heard the chik-chik-chik of crickets. I sat up in bed and shut the window and turned the metal lock on top.

I had heard tales of other voyages, out beyond the ends of the town, high up into the clouds. Joey knew a boy who'd gone up so high you couldn't see him any more, like a balloon that grows smaller and smaller and vanishes – as if suddenly – into blue regions beyond the reach of sight. There were towns up there, so they said; I didn't know; white cloud-towns, with towers. Up there, in the blue beyond the blue, there were rivers you could go under the way you could walk under a bridge; birds with rainbow-coloured tails; ice mountains and cities of snow; flattened shining masses of light like whirling discs; blue gardens; slow-moving creatures with leathery wings; towns inhabited by the dead. My father had taught me not to believe stories about Martians and spaceships, and these tales were like those stories: even as you refused to believe them, you saw them, as if the sheer effort of not believing them made them glow in your mind. Beside such stories, my forbidden night journey over the rooftops seemed tame as a stroll. I could feel dark desires ripening within me; stubbornly I returned to my old games, as carpets moved in backyards, forming bars of red and green across white shingles.

Came a day when my mother let me stay home while she went shopping at the market at the top of the hill. I wanted to call out after her: stop! make me go with you! I saw her walking across the lawn towards the open garage. My father had taken the bus to work. In my room I raised the blinds and looked out at the brilliant blue sky. For a long time I looked at that sky before unlocking the window, pushing up the glass and screen.

I set forth high over the backyard and rose smoothly into the blue. I kept my eyes ahead and up, though now and then I let my gaze fall over the carpet's edge. Down below I saw little red and black roofs, the shadows of houses thrown all on one side, a sunny strip of road fringed with sharp-bent tree-shadows, as if they had been blown sideways by a wind – and here and there, on neat squares of lawn, little carpets flying above their moving shadows. The sky was blue, pure blue. When I next glanced down I saw white puffballs hanging motionless over factory smokestacks, oil tanks like white coins by a glittering brown river. Up above, in all that blue, I saw only a small white cloud, with a little rip at the bottom, as if someone had started to tear it in half. The empty sky was so blue, so richly and thickly blue, that it seemed a thing I ought to be able to feel, like lake water or snow. I had read a story once about a boy who walked into a lake and came to a town on the bottom, and now it seemed to me that I was plunging deep into a lake, even though I was climbing. Below me I saw a misty patch of cloud, rectangles of dark green and butterscotch and brown. The blue stretched above like fields of snow, like fire. I imagined myself standing in my yard, looking up at my carpet growing smaller and smaller until it vanished into blue. I felt myself vanishing into blue. He was vanishing into blue. Below my carpet I saw only blue. In this blue beyond blue, all nothing everywhere, was I still I? I had passed out of sight, the string holding me to earth had snapped, and in these realms of blue I saw no rivers and white towns, no fabulous birds, but only shimmering distances of skyblue heavenblue blue. In that blaze of blue I tried to remember whether the boy in the lake had ever come back; and looking down at that ungraspable blue, which plunged away on both sides, I longed for the hardness under green grass, tree bark scraping my back, sidewalks, dark stones. Maybe it was the fear of never coming back, maybe it was the blue passing into me and soaking me through and through, but a dizziness came over me, I closed my eyes – and it seemed to me that I was falling through the sky, that my carpet had blown away, that the rush of my falling had knocked the wind out of me, that I had died, was about to die, as in a dream when I felt myself falling towards the sharp rocks, that I was running, tumbling, crawling, pursued by blue; and opening my eyes I saw that I had come down within sight of housetops, my hands clutching the edges of my carpet like claws. I swooped lower and soon recognized the rooftops of my neighbourhood. There was Joey's yard, there was my garden, there was my chicken coop, my swing; and landing in the yard I felt the weight of the earth streaming up through me like a burst of joy.

At dinner I could scarcely keep my eyes open. By bedtime I had a temperature. There were no fits of coughing, no itchy eyes, or raw red lines under runny nostrils – only a steady burning, a heavy weariness, lasting three days. In my bed, under the covers, behind closed blinds, I lay reading a book that kept falling forward onto my chest. On the fourth day I woke feeling alert and cool-skinned. My mother, who for three days had been lowering her hand gently to my forehead and staring at me with grave, searching eyes, now walked briskly about the room, opening blinds with a sharp thin sound, drawing them up with a clatter. In the morning I was allowed to play quietly in the yard. In the afternoon I stood behind my mother on an escalator leading up to boys' pants. School was less than two weeks away; I had outgrown everything; Grandma was coming up for a visit; Joey's uncle had brought real horseshoes with him; there was no time, no time for anything at all; and as I walked to school along hot sidewalks shaded by maples, along the sandy roadside past Ciccarelli's lot, up Franklin Street and along Collins Street, I saw, in the warm and summery September air, like a gigantic birthmark, a brilliant patch of red leaves among the green.

One rainy day when I was in my room looking for a slipper, I found my rolled-up carpet under the bed. Fluffs of dust stuck to it like bees. Irritably I lugged it down into the cellar and laid it on top of an old trunk under the stairs. On a snowy afternoon in January I chased a ping-pong ball into the light-striped darkness under the cellar stairs. Long spiderwebs like delicate rigging had grown in the dark space, stretching from the rims of barrels to the undersides of the steps. My old carpet lay on the crumbly floor between the trunk and a wooden barrel. 'I've got it!' I cried, seizing the white ball with its sticky little clump of spiderweb, rubbing it clean with my thumb, bending low as I ducked back into the yellow light of the cellar. The sheen on the dark green table made it look silky. Through a high window I could see the snow slanting down, falling steadily, piling up against the glass.

The new automaton theatre

Our city is justly proud of its automaton theatre. By this I do not mean simply that the difficult and exacting art of the automaton is carried by our masters to a pitch of brilliance unequalled elsewhere and unimagined by the masters of an earlier age. Rather I mean that by its very nature our automaton theatre is deserving of pride, for it is the source of our richest and most spiritual pleasure. We know that without it our lives would lack something, though we cannot say with any certainty what it is that we would lack. And we are proud that ours is a genuinely popular theatre, commanding the fervent loyalty of young and old alike. It is scarcely an exaggeration to say that from the moment we emerge from the cradle we fall under an enchantment from which we never awake. So pronounced is our devotion, which some call an obsession, that common wisdom distinguishes four separate phases. In childhood we are said to be attracted by the colour and movement of these little creatures, in adolescence by the intricate clockwork mechanisms that give them the illusion of life, in adulthood by the truth and beauty of the dramas they enact, and in old age by the timeless perfection of an art that lifts us above the cares of mortality and gives meaning to our lives. Such distinctions are recognized by everyone to be fanciful, yet in their own way they express a truth. For like our masters, who pass from a long apprenticeship to ever-greater heights of achievement, we too pass from the apprenticeship of childish delight to the graver pleasures of a mature and discriminating enjoyment. No one ever outgrows the automaton theatre.

It must be confessed that the precise number of our theatres remains unknown, for not only are they springing up continually, but many of the lesser companies travel from hall to hall without benefit of permanent lodging. The masters themselves may exhibit at a single hall, or in several at once. It is generally agreed that well over eight hundred theatres are in operation throughout our city in the course of a single year; and there is no day during which one cannot attend some hundred performances.

Despite a great number of books on the subject, the origin of the automaton theatre is shrouded in darkness. From the singing birds of Hero of Alexandria to Vaucanson's duck, every item of clockwork ingenuity has by some authority been cited as an influence; nor have historians failed to lay tribute to the art of Byzantium. Some scholars have gone so far as to lend a questionable authority to Johann Müller's fly, which legend tells us was able to alight on the hands of all the guests seated in a room before returning to its maker. Yet even if such tales should prove to be true, they would fail to explain our own more elegant art, which not only exceeds the crude imaginings of legend but is entirely explicable and demonstrable. One theory has it that our earliest clockwork artisans – about whom, it is admitted, little is known – were directly influenced by the doll's-house art of medieval Nürnberg, a conjecture to which a certain weight is lent by church records showing that fourteen of our ancestors were born in Nürnberg. What is certain is that the art of the miniature has long flourished in our town, and quite independently of the automaton theatre. No home is without its cherrystone basket, its peachpit troll; and the splendid Hall of Miniatures in our Stadtmuseum is widely known. Yet I would argue that it is precisely our admirable miniatures which reveal their essential difference from our automaton theatre. In the Stadtmuseum one can see such marvels of the miniature art as an ark carved from the pit of a cherry, containing three dozen pairs of clearly distinguishable animals, as well as Noah and his sons; and carved from a piece of boxwood one inch long and displayed beneath a magnifying lens, the winter palace of the Hohenzollerns, with its topiary garden, its orchard of pear trees and its many rooms, containing more than three hundred pieces of precise furniture. But when one has done admiring the skill of such miniature masterworks, one cannot fail to be struck by their difference from our automaton theatre. In the first place, although it is called a miniature theatre, these six-inch figures that lend such enchantment to our lives are virtual giants in comparison with the true masterpieces of miniature art. In the second place, the art of the miniature is in essence a lifeless art, an art of stillness, whereas the art of the automaton lies above all in the creation of living motion. Yet having said as much, I do not mean to deny all relation between the miniatures of our museums and the exquisite internal structures – the clockwork souls – of our automatons.

Although the origin of our art is obscure and the precise lines of its development difficult to unravel, there is no doubt concerning the tendency of the art during the long course of its distinguished history. That tendency is towards an ever-increasing mastery of the illusion of life. The masterpieces of eighteenth-century clockwork art preserved in our museums are not without a charm and beauty of their own, but in the conquest of motion they can in no way compare to the products of the current age. The art has advanced so rapidly that even our apprentices of twelve exceed the earliest masters, for they can produce figures capable of executing more than five hundred separate motions; and it is well known that in the last two generations our own masters have conquered in their automatons every motion of which a human being is capable. Thus the mechanical challenge inherent in our art has been met and mastered.

Yet such is the nature of our art that the mechanical is intimately related to the spiritual. It is precisely the brilliance of our advance in clockwork that has enabled our masters to express the full beauty of living human form. Every gesture of the human body, every shade of emotion that expresses itself on a human face, is captured in the mobile forms and features of our miniature automatons. It has even been argued that these finely wrought creatures are capable of expressing in their faces certain deep and complex emotions which the limited human musculature can never hope to achieve. Those who blame our art for too great a reliance on mechanical ingenuity (for we are not without our critics) would do well to consider the relation between the physical and the spiritual, and to ask themselves whether the most poetic feeling in the soul of man can exist without the prosaic agency of a nervous system.

By its nature, then, our art is mimetic; and each advance has been a new encroachment on the preserves of life. Visitors who see our automatons for the first time are awed and even disturbed by their lifelike qualities. Truly our figures seem to think and breathe. But having acknowledged the mimetic or illusionistic tendency of our art, I hasten to point out that the realism of which I speak must not be misunderstood to mean the narrow and constricting sort that dominates and deadens our literature. It is a realism of means, which in no way excludes the fanciful. There is first of all the traditional distinction between the Children's Theatre and the theatre proper. In the Children's Theatre we find as many witches, dragons, ghosts and walking trees as may delight the imagination of the most implacable dreamer; but they are, if I may risk a paradox, real witches, real dragons, real ghosts and real walking trees. In these figures, all the resources of clockwork art are brought to bear in the precise and perfected expression of the impossible. The real is used to bring forth the unreal. It is a mimesis of the fantastic, a scrupulous rendering of creatures who differ from real creatures solely by their quality of inexistence. But even the adult theatre is by no means to be measured by the laughable banalities of our so-called realistic literature. For here too we can point to a great and pleasing variety of theatrical forms, which have evolved along with the evolving art of clockwork and which are limited only by the special nature of the art itself. Being a speechless art, it relies entirely on a subtle expressivity of gesture – an apparent limitation that, in the hands of our masters, becomes the very means of its greatness. For these performances, which run from twenty to forty minutes and are accompanied by such musical effects as may be required, seek no less than music itself to express the inexpressible and give precise and lasting shape to the deepest impulses of the human spirit. Thus some dramas may suggest the ballet, others the mime, still others the silent cinema; yet their form is their own entirely, various as the imagination, but all betraying a secret kinship.

But even aside from the great variety of our automaton theatre, this most realistic and mechanical of arts, which strives for an absolute imitation of Nature, cannot be called realistic without serious qualification. For in the first place, the automatons are but six inches high. This fact alone makes nonsense of the charge that our art is narrowly realistic in spirit and intention. The vogue of life-sized automatons, current some years ago, quite passed us by. Well known is the response evoked by the gross automatons of Count Orsini, upon the occasion of that worthy's much advertised visit to our city. One imagines the howls of laughter still ringing in his ears. But quite apart from the small size of our automatons is the nature of the pleasure of automaton art itself. It would be foolish to deny that this pleasure is in part a pleasure of imitation, of likeness. It is the pleasure of illusion fully mastered. But precisely this pleasure depends on a second pleasure, which is opposed to the first; or it may be that the pleasure of imitation is itself divisible into two opposing parts. This second pleasure, or this second half of the pleasure of imitation, is a pleasure of unlikeness. With secret joy we perceive every way in which the illusion is not the thing itself, but only an illusion; and this pleasure increases as the illusion itself becomes more compelling. For we are not children, we do not forget we are at the theatre. The naturalness of the creatures moving and suffering on their little stage only increases our reverence for the masters who brought them into being.

These masters, of whom there are never more than twenty or thirty in a generation, are themselves the highest expression of a rigorous system of training that even on its lower levels is capable of producing works of superb skill and enchanting beauty; yet it is notable that despite occasional proposals the method has never cohered into a formal school. In somewhat arbitrary fashion the masters continue to take on apprentices, who move into the workshops and are expected to devote themselves exclusively to their art. Many of course cannot endure the rigours of such a life, which in addition to being narrow and arduous does not even hold out the promise of future prosperity. For it remains curiously true that despite public fervour the masters are, if not impecunious, at any rate far from prosperous. Many reasons have been adduced for this shameful state of affairs, one of the more fanciful being that the masters are so dedicated to their art that external comfort leaves them indifferent. But this can hardly be the case. The masters are not monks; they marry, they have children, they are responsible for maintaining a family with the additional burden of apprentices, not all of whom can pay even for their food. They are human beings like everyone else, with all the cares of suffering humanity, in addition to the burden of their rigorous art. Indeed the grave and sorrowing features of the older masters seem witness of a secret unhappiness. And so a far more plausible explanation of their lack of prosperity is that the laboriousness of the art far exceeds its capacity to pay. The theatres flourish, money pours in; but the construction of a single clockwork figure takes from six months to two or more years. Of course the masters are aided in large part by the higher apprentices, who are permitted to construct hands and feet, and even entire legs and arms, as well as the clockwork mechanisms of the less expressive portions of the anatomy. Yet even so the master automatist is entirely responsible for the face and head, and the final adjustments of the whole. And although the painting of the scenery on translucent linen – itself a labour of many months – is left almost entirely to the older apprentices, nevertheless the master automatist must provide the original sketches; and the same is true of many other matters, such as the elaborate lighting that, illuminating the beautiful translucencies, is so much a part of our automaton theatre. And of course there is the drama itself, the choreography, the sometimes elaborate music. For all these reasons, our daily attendance at the theatres does not lead to prosperity for the masters, though the theatre managers invariably live in the best part of town.

The mechanical skill of the masters, their profound understanding of the secrets of clockwork art, is impressive and even unsettling; but mechanical genius alone does not make a master. That this is so is evident from the fact that some apprentices as early as their thirteenth year are able to construct an automaton whose motions are anatomically flawless. Yet they are far from being masters, for their creatures lack that mysterious quality which makes the true masterpieces of our art seem to think and suffer and breathe. It is true that anatomical perfection is a high level of accomplishment and suffices for the Children's Theatre. Yet when these same apprentices, impatient to be recognized, attempt several years later to start theatres of their own, the lack of spiritual mastery is immediately evident and they are forced either to resign themselves to a life of service in the Children's Theatre or else to return to the rigours of the higher apprenticeship. Even among those recognized as masters there are perceptible differences of accomplishment, though at a level so high that comparisons tend to take the form of arguments concerning the nature of beauty. Yet it may happen that one master stands out from the others by virtue of some scarcely to be defined yet immediately apparent quality, as our history demonstrates again and again; and as is the case at present, in the disquieting instance of Heinrich Graum.

For it is indeed of him that I wish to speak, this troubled spirit who has risen up in our midst with his perilous and disturbing gift; and if I have seemed to hesitate, to linger over other matters, it is because the very nature of his art throws all into question and requires one to approach him obliquely, almost warily.

Like many masters, Heinrich Graum was the son of a watchmaker; like most, he displayed his gift early. At the age of five he was sent to the workshop of Rudolf Eisenmann, from which so many apprentices emerge as young masters. There he proved a talented but not precocious pupil. At the age of seven he constructed a one-inch nightingale capable of sixty-four motions, including thirty-six separate motions of the head, and exhibiting such perfect craftsmanship that it was used in the orchard scene of Eisenmann's *Der Reisende Kavalier*. This was followed almost a year later by a charming high-wire artist who climbed to the top of his post, walked with the aid of a balancing pole across the wire towards the opposite post, lost and regained his balance three times, fell and clung to the wire with one hand, climbed laboriously back up and continued safely to the opposite post, where he turned and bowed. In all this there was nothing to distinguish young Heinrich from any talented apprentice; he was never a child prodigy, as has since mistakenly been claimed. A far greater degree of precocity is very frequent among the child apprentices and is looked upon by the masters with a certain distrust. For in an art that more than any other demands a thorough mastery of mechanical details, a too-early success often leads the young apprentice to a false sense of ripeness. All too often the prodigy of seven is the mediocrity of fifteen, fit only for service in the Children's Theatre. For it is not too much to say that the highest form of the automatist's art is entirely spiritual, though attained, as I have said, by mechanical means. The child prodigies display a remarkable technical virtuosity that is certainly impressive but that does not in itself give promise of future greatness, and that more often than not distracts them and other apprentices from their proper path of development. Young Heinrich was spared the affliction of precocity.

But he was highly talented; and a master always watches his talented apprentices for any sign of that indefinable quality which marks a pupil as doomed to mastery. In the case of young Heinrich it was his early interest in the human form and above all in the hands and face. At precisely the time when talented apprentices of ten and twelve are turning their attention to the dragons and mermaids of the Children's Theatre, and revelling in the display of their considerable technical skills, Heinrich began to study the inner structure of Eisenmann's famous magician, capable of making a silver coin disappear, producing a bluebird from his hat, and shuffling and holding outspread in his hands a deck of fifty-two miniature cards. It was the mechanical problem that appears to have engaged young Heinrich's interest; it was the first problem he could not solve rapidly. For eight months during his twelfth year he dissected and reassembled the hands of the anatomical models that flourish in every workshop; the intricate clockwork structure of the thumb appears to have obsessed him. And in this too he distinguished himself from the child wonders, who move rapidly and a little breathlessly from one accomplishment to the next. At the end of eight months he was able to construct the precise duplicate of Eisenmann's magician – a feat that earned him the master's first serious attention. But what is more remarkable is that young Heinrich was still dissatisfied. He continued to study the structure of the hand (his series of sixty-three hands from this period is considered by some to be his first mature work) and shortly before his fourteenth birthday produced an Eisenmann magician capable of three new tricks never attempted before in automaton art. One of these tricks achieved a certain notoriety when it was discovered that no human magician was capable of duplicating it. Young Heinrich confessed to having improved the musculature of the hand beyond a merely human capacity; for this he was lightly rebuked.

The magician was followed quickly by his first original creation, the astonishing pianist capable of playing the entire first movement of the Moonlight Sonata on a beautifully constructed seven-inch grand piano. Heinrich had only a slight musical training and the execution of the movement left much to be desired, but all agreed that the hands of the pianist displayed the mark of a future master.

Heinrich at fourteen was a large, slumped, serious boy, whose thick-fingered hands looked clumsy in comparison with the delicate clockwork hands of his creatures. Aside from his taciturnity, which even then was notable, he was in no way sullen or eccentric, as so many talented apprentices prove to be, and among his peers he had an unusual reputation for kindness. He seems to have slid awkwardly but without a struggle into young manhood, wearing his large and powerful body with an air of surprise.

It was immediately after the completion of the pianist that he began the study of the human face which was to have such profound consequences for his art and to make of him an acknowledged master by the age of twenty. For six long years he analysed and dissected the automaton face, studying the works of the masters and trying to penetrate the deepest secrets of expressivity. During this entire period he completed not a single figure, but instead accumulated a gallery of some six hundred heads, many of them in grotesque states of incompletion. Eisenmann recognized the signs of maturing mastership and allowed the stooped, grave youth to have his way. At the end of the six-year period Heinrich created in two feverish months the first figure since his pianist: the young woman whom he called Fräulein Elise.

Eisenmann himself pronounced it a masterpiece, and even now we may admire it as a classic instance of automaton art. This charming figure, who measures scarcely five inches in height, moves with a grace and naturalness that are the surest signs of mastership. Her famous walk, so indolently sensual, would alone have ensured the young master a place in the histories. She seems the very essence of girlhood passing into womanhood. But even in this early figure one is struck above all by the startling expressivity of the face. During her twelve minutes of clockwork life, Fräulein Elise appears to be undergoing a spiritual struggle, every shadow of which is displayed in her intelligent features. She paces her room now restlessly, now indolently, throwing herself onto her bed, gazing out the window, sitting up abruptly, falling into a muse. We seem to be drawn into the very soul of this girl, troubled as she is with the vague yearnings and dark intuitions of innocence on the threshold of knowledge. Every perfectly rendered gesture seems designed only to draw us more deeply inwards; we feel an uncanny intimacy with this restless creature, whose mysterious life we seem to know more deeply than our own. The long, languorous, slowly unfolding, darkly yearning yawn that concludes the performance, as Elise appears to open like a heavy blossom and draw us into the depths of her being, is a masterpiece of spiritual penetration, all the more remarkable in that Heinrich is not known to have been in love at this time. One fellow apprentice, a thin youth of eighteen, was so stirred by Elise that he was observed to study her twelve-minute life again and again. As the weeks passed his cheeks grew pale, a dark blueness appeared below his eyes; and it was said that he had fallen in love with the little Fräulein Elise.

The young master now entered upon a period of powerful creativity, which in four years' time led to his first public performance. The success of the Zaubertheater was immediate and decisive. His figures were compared to the greatest masterpieces of clockwork art; all commentators remarked upon their supple expressivity, their uncanny intensity. Here was an artist who at the age of twenty-four had not only mastered the subtlest intricacies of clockwork motion but, in an art where innovation was often disastrous and always dangerous, had added something genuinely new. No one could ignore the haunting 'inwardness' of his admirable creatures; it was as if Heinrich Graum had learned to shadow forth emotions never seen before. Even those who disdained all innovation as inherently destructive were compelled to offer their grudging admiration, for when all was said and done the young master had simply carried the art one step further in the honourable direction of scrupulous imitation. His difference was noted and admired by those of most exacting taste; and he was pronounced to be in the classic tradition of the great masters, though with a distinctive modern flavour peculiarly and compellingly his own. Thus did it come about that he was admired equally by the older generation and the new.

It is one thing for a young master to earn his reputation; it is another for him to sustain it. Heinrich Graum was not one to ignore a challenge. In the course of the next twelve years the grave young master seemed to surpass himself with every new composition, each one of which was awaited with an eagerness bordering on fever. Audiences responded in kind to the peculiar intensity of his creatures; young women especially were susceptible to the strange power that glowed in those clockwork eyes. Well known is the case of Ilse Länger, who fell so desperately in love with his dark-eyed Pierrot that the mere sight of him would cause her to burst into fits of violent sobbing. One rainy Sunday, after a tormented night, the suffering girl left her house before dawn, walked along the gloomy avenue of elms north of the Schlosspark and threw herself into the Bree, leaving behind a pitiful love note and the fragment of a poem. Poor Ilse Länger was only an extreme and unfortunate instance of a widespread phenomenon. The tears of women were not uncommon at the Zaubertheater; young men wrote fiery poems to his Klara. Even sober critics were not above responses of the extreme kind, which sometimes troubled them and which served as the basis of an occasional attack. It was noted that Graum's figures seemed more and more to be pushing at the limits of the human, as if he wished to express in his creatures not only the deepest secrets of the human soul but emotions that lay beyond the knowledge of men; and this sense of excess, which was at the very heart of his greatness, was itself seen to pose a danger, for it was said that his figures walked a narrow line dividing them from the grotesque. But such attacks, inevitable in an art of high and ancient tradition, were little more than a murmur in the thunder of serious applause; and the performances at the Zaubertheater were soon being called the triumph of the age, the final and richest flowering of the automatist's art.

It was perhaps the very extremity of these well-deserved claims that should have given us pause, for if an art has indeed been carried to its richest expression, then we may wonder whether the urge that impelled it in the direction of its fulfilment may not impel it beyond its proper limit. In this sense we may ask whether the highest form of an art contains within it the elements of its own destruction – whether decadence, in short, so far from being the sickly opposite of art's deepest health, is perhaps nothing but the result of an urge identical to both.

However that may be, the young master continued to move from triumph to triumph, shocking us with the revelation of ever-new spiritual depths, and making us yearn for darker and deeper beauties. It was as if his creatures strained at the very limits of the human, without leaving the human altogether; and the intensity of his late figures seemed to promise some final vision, which we awaited with longing and a little dread.

It was at the age of thirty-six, after twelve years of uninterrupted triumph, that Heinrich Graum suddenly fell silent.

Now the silence of masters is not unusual and is in itself no cause for alarm. It is well known that the masters undergo great and continual strain, for when we speak of mastering the sublime art of the automaton we do not mean a mastery that leads to relaxation of effort. It may indeed with more truth be said that the achievement of mastery is only the necessary preparation for future rigours. How else are we to explain the grave, melancholy countenances of our masters? The high art of the automaton demands a relentless and unremitting precision, an unwavering power of concentration and a ceaseless faculty for invention, so that mastery itself must always struggle merely to maintain its own level. In addition there is the never acknowledged but always felt presence of the other masters. For there is a secret rivalry among them. Each feels the presence of the others, against whom he measures himself mercilessly; and although it may be that such rivalry is harmful to the health of the masters, yet without it there is every likelihood that the art would suffer, for a faint and scarcely conscious relaxation would inevitably set in. In addition to this rivalry, each master is a rival of the great masters of the past; and each is also a rival of himself, continually striving to surpass his own most superb achievements. Such pressures are more than sufficient to engrave deep lines on the faces of our masters, but there are in addition the continual threat of poverty, the burden of having to live in two worlds at once, and the common lot of suffering that no mortal can escape and that often seems to the master, stretched as he always is to the highest pitch of a strained and exacting creativity, too much to bear. Thus it comes about that a master will sometimes fall into silence, from which he will emerge in six months or a year or two years as if born anew, while in his absence the theatre is run by his leading apprentices. The striking feature of Heinrich Graum's case is therefore not the silence itself, nor even the suddenness of the silence, but rather its thoroughness and duration. For Graum remained silent for ten long years; and unlike all other masters who temporarily retire, he closed his theatre and withdrew all his creatures from public performance.

The debate over the ten-year silence of Heinrich Graum will in all probability never cease. It has been compared in some quarters to Schiller's twelve-year silence between *Don Carlos* and *Wallenstein*, but perhaps I may be permitted to point out that Schiller began to compose poetry (if not drama) eight years after the completion of *Don Carlos*, that he worked steadily on *Wallenstein* from 1797 to 1799 and that in any case he was far from silent, since he published two full-length histories as well as numerous philosophical and aesthetic essays during the very years of his dramatic silence. Graum's silence was complete. Moreover he released his apprentices. We have therefore no witnesses of his activity during this decisive period. He had married quietly during the triumphant years and there is no cause whatever for connecting his silence in any way with his domestic life. During his silent years he is known to have made several trips in the company of his wife to various bathing resorts on the Nordsee; he was twice seen in a chair on the beach at Scheveningen, a stooped giant of a man in brown bathing trunks, staring out gloomily at the water. But most of the time he appears to have remained shut up in his workshop on the Lindenallee. It is commonly assumed that there he tirelessly took apart and recomposed clockwork creatures in the manner of his obsessive youth. Nothing can be proved to the contrary, for he has remained silent about this as about all other matters, but against the general assumption two objections may briefly be raised. First, no trace of any automaton from this period has ever been found. Second, the nature of the new automaton theatre renders the theory of ceaseless experiment unlikely. It may be argued that he destroyed all his experiments; yet it should be remembered that he carefully preserved the sixty-three hands and more than six hundred heads of his apprenticeship. My own suggestion, which I offer after long and serious reflection, is that for ten years Heinrich Graum did nothing. Or to be more precise: he did nothing, while thinking ceaselessly about the nature of his art. Had he been a man of letters, a Schiller, he might have offered to the world the fruits of his meditations; his genius being of the wordless kind, his thoughts were reflected only in the strange creatures that suddenly burst from him towards the end of this period, changing the nature of our automaton theatre forever.

When the Zaubertheater first closed, we were disappointed and expectant. As the silence continued, our expectation diminished, while our disappointment grew. In time even our disappointment faded, returning only in stray eruptions of sadness or, on lavender summer evenings when the yellow street lamps came on, a vague uneasiness, a restlessness, as if we were searching for something that had departed forever.

Meanwhile we threw ourselves into the automaton theatre. It

was a time of ripeness in the art; and it was said that never before had the skill of so many masters reached such a pitch of expressive brilliance, haunted as they all were by the memory of the old Zaubertheater.

The rumour of the great master's return was at first greeted with a certain reserve. He had vanished so completely that his possible reappearance among us was somehow disturbing. It was as if a beloved son, ten years dead, should suddenly return, long after one had made one's thousand little accommodations. An entire generation of apprentices had entered the workshops without having seen a single work of the legendary master; some were openly sceptical. Even we who had mourned his silence were secretly uncertain, for we had grown accustomed to things as they were, we had lost the habit of genius. In our timid hearts, did we not pray that he would stay away? Yet as the day drew near we became tense with expectancy; and in our pulses we could feel, like an eruption of fever at the onset of an unknown disease, a slow, secret excitement.

And Heinrich Graum returned; again the old Zaubertheater opened its doors. That long-awaited performance was like a knife flashed in the face of our art. Of those who remained during the full thirty-six minutes, some were openly enraged, others sickened and ashamed; a few were seized by the roots of the soul, though in a manner they could not understand and later refused to discuss. One critic stated that the master had lost his mind; others, more kindly though no more accurately, spoke of parody and the grotesque. Even now one still hears such charges and descriptions; the Neues Zaubertheater remains at the centre of a passionate controversy. Those who do not share our love of the automaton theatre may find our passions difficult to understand; but for us it was as if everything had suddenly been thrown into question. Even we who have been won over are disturbed by these performances, which trouble us like forbidden pleasures, like secret crimes.

I have spoken of the long and noble history of our art, and of its tendency towards an ever-increasing mimetic brilliance. Young Heinrich had inherited this tradition, and in the opinion of many had become its outstanding master. In one stroke his Neues Zaubertheater stood history on its head. The new automatons can only be described as clumsy. By this I mean that the smoothness of motion so characteristic of our classic figures has been replaced by the jerky abrupt motions of amateur automatons. As a result the new automatons cannot imitate the motions of human beings, except in the most elementary way. They lack grace; by every rule of classic automaton art they are inept and ugly. They do not strike us as human. Indeed it must be said that the new automatons strike us first of all *as automatons*. This is the essence of what has come to be called The New Automaton Theatre.

I have called the new automatons clumsy, and this is true enough if we judge them from the standpoint of the master-pieces of the older school. But it is not entirely true, judged even from that standpoint. In the first place, the clumsiness itself is extremely artful, as imitators have learned to their cost. It is not a matter of simply reducing the number of motions, but of reducing them in a particular way, so that a particular rhythm of motions is produced. In the second place, the acknowledged master of expressivity cannot be said to have turned against the expressive itself. The new automatons are profoundly expressive in their own disturbing way. Indeed it has been noticed that the new automatons are capable of motions never seen before in the automatist's art, although it is a matter of dispute whether these motions may properly be called human.

In the classic automaton theatre we are asked to share the emotions of human beings, whom in reality we know to be miniature automatons. In the new automaton theatre we are asked to share the emotions of automatons themselves. The clockwork artifice, far from being disguised, is thrust upon our attention. If this were all, it would be startling, but it would not be much. Such a theatre could not last. But Graum's new automatons suffer and struggle; no less than the old automatons do they appear to have souls. But they do not have the souls of human beings; they have the souls of clockwork creatures, grown conscious of themselves. The classic automatists present us with miniature people; Heinrich Graum has invented a new race. They are the race of automatons, the clan of clockwork; they are new beings, inserted into the universe by the mind of Graum the creator. They live lives that are parallel to ours but are not to be confused with ours. Their struggles are clockwork struggles, their suffering is the suffering of automatons.

It has become fashionable of late to claim that Graum abandoned the adult theatre and returned to the Children's Theatre as to his spiritual home. To my mind this is a gross misunderstanding. The creatures of the Children's Theatre are imitations of imaginary beings; Graum's creatures are not imitations of anything. They are only themselves. Dragons do not exist; automatons do.

In this sense Graum's revolution may be seen to be a radical continuation of our history rather than a reversal or rejection of it. I have said that our art is realistic and that all advances in the technical realm have been in the service of the real. Graum's new automatons offer no less homage to Nature. For him, human beings are one thing and clockwork creatures another; to confuse the two is to propagate the unreal.

Art, a master once observed, is never theoretical. My laborious remarks obscure the delicate art they seek to elucidate. Nothing short of attendance at the Neues Zaubertheater can convey the startling, disturbing quality of the new automatons. We seem drawn into the souls of these creatures, who assert their unreal nature at every jerk of a limb; we suffer their clumsiness, we are pierced by inhuman longings. We are moved in ways we can

scarcely comprehend. We yearn to mingle with these strange
newcomers, to pass into their clockwork lives; at times we feel a
dark understanding, a criminal complicity. Is it that in their
presence we are able to shed the merely human, which seems a
limitation, and to release ourselves into a larger, darker, more
dangerous realm? We know only that we are stirred in places
untouched before. A dark, disturbing beauty, like a black
sunrise, has come into our lives. Dying of a thirst we did not
know we had, we drink from the necessary and tormenting
waters of fictive fountains.

And the new automatons begin to obsess us. They penetrate
our minds, they multiply within us, they inhabit our dreams.
They waken in us new, forbidden passions we cannot name.
Once again it is adolescent girls who have proved to be
peculiarly susceptible to Graum's dark wizardry. In any audience one can see three or four of them, with their parted lips,
their hungry eyes, their tense, hysterical attention. The tears
that flow are not the tears of love, but quite different tears, deep,
scalding tears torn up from unspeakable depths, tears that give
no relief, tears wrung from nerves tormented by the crystalline
harmonies of unearthly violins. Even our stern young men
emerge from these dangerous performances with haunted eyes.
Incidents of a pathological kind have been reported; the
demonic pact between Wolfgang Kohler and Eva Holst must be
passed over in silence. More troubling because more common
are the taut, drained faces one sees after certain performances,
especially after the terrifying dissolution scene in *Die Neue Elise*.
The new art is not a gentle art; its beauties are of an almost
unbearable intensity.

These are perhaps superficial signs; more profound is the new
restlessness one feels in our city, an impatience with older
forms, a secret hunger.

They are no longer the same, the old automatons. Gratefully
we seek out the old theatres, but once we have felt the troubling

touch of the new automatons we find ourselves growing impatient with the smooth and perfect motions of the old masters, whose brilliant imitations seem to us nothing but clockwork confections. So, rather guiltily, we return to the Neues Zaubertheater, where the new automatons draw us into their inhuman joys and sufferings, and fill us with uneasy rapture. The old art flourishes, and its presence comforts us, but something new and strange has come into the world. We may try to explain it, but what draws us is the mystery. For our dreams have changed. Whether our art has fallen into an unholy decadence, as many have charged, or whether it has achieved its deepest and darkest flowering, who among us can say? We know only that nothing can ever be the same.

Clair de lune

The summer I turned fifteen, I could no longer fall asleep. I would lie motionless on my back, in a perfect imitation of sleep, and imagine myself lying fast asleep with my head turned to one side and a tendon pushed up along the skin of my neck, but even as I watched myself lying there dead to the world I could hear the faint burr of my electric clock, a sharp creak in the attic – like a single footstep – a low rumbling hum that I knew was the sound of trucks rolling along the distant throughway. I could feel the collar of my pyjama top touching my jaw. Through my trembling eyelids I sensed that the darkness of the night was not dark enough and, suddenly opening my eyes, as if to catch someone in my room, I'd see the moonlight streaming past the edges of the closed venetian blinds.

I could make out the lampshade and bent neck of the standing lamp, like a great drooping black sunflower. On the floor by a bookcase the white king and part of a black bishop glowed on the moon-striped chessboard. My room was filling up with moonlight. The darkness I longed for, the darkness that had once sheltered me, had been pushed into corners, where it lay in thick, furry lumps. I felt a heaviness in my chest, an oppression – I wanted to hide in the dark. Desperately I closed my eyes, imagining the blackness of a winter night: snow covered the silent streets, on the front porch the ice chopper stood leaning next to the black mailbox glinting with icicles, lines of snow lay along the cross-pieces of telephone poles and the tops of metal street signs: and always through my eyelids I could feel the summer moonlight pushing back the dark.

One night I sat up in bed harshly and threw the covers off. My eyes burned from sleeplessness. I could no longer stand this nightly violation of the dark. I dressed quietly, tensely, since my parents' room stood on the other side of my two bookcases, then made my way along the hall and out into the living-room. A stripe of moonlight lay across a couch cushion. On the music rack I could see a pattern of black notes on the moon-streaked pages of Debussy's 'Second Arabesque', which my mother had left off practising that evening. In a deep ashtray shaped like a shell the bowl of my father's pipe gleamed like a piece of obsidian.

At the front door I hesitated a moment, then stepped out into the warm summer night.

The sky surprised me. It was deep blue, the blue of a sorcerer's hat, of night skies in old Technicolor movies, of deep mountain lakes in Swiss countrysides pictured on old puzzle boxes. I remembered my father removing from a leather pouch in his camera bag a circle of silver and handing it to me, and when I held it up I saw through the dark blue glass a dark blue world the colour of this night. Suddenly I stepped out of the shadow of the house into the whiteness of the moon. The moon was so bright I could not look at it, as if it were a night sun. The fierce whiteness seemed hot, but for some reason I thought of the glittering thick frost on the inside of the ice-cream freezer in a barely remembered store: the popsicles and ice-cream cups crusted in ice crystals, the cold air like steam.

I could smell low tide in the air and thought of heading for the beach, but I found myself walking the other way. For already I knew where I was going, knew and did not know where I was going, in the sorcerer-blue night where all things were changed, and as I passed the neighbouring ranch houses I took in the chimney-shadows black and sharp across the roofs, the television antennas standing clean and hard against the blue night sky.

Soon the ranch houses gave way to small two-storey houses, the smell of the tide was gone. The shadows of telephone wires showed clearly on the moonwashed streets. The wire-shadows looked like curved musical staves. On a brilliant white garage door the slanting, intricate shadow of a basketball net reminded me of the rigging on the wooden ship model I had built with my father, one childhood summer. I could not understand why no one was out on a night like this. Was I the only one who'd been drawn out of hiding and heaviness by the summer moon? In an open, empty garage I saw cans of moonlit paint on a shelf, an aluminium ladder hanging on hooks, folded lawn chairs. Under the big-leafed maples moonlight rippled across my hands.

Oh, I knew where I was going, didn't want to know where I was going, in the warm blue air with little flutters of coolness in it, little bursts of grass-smell and leaf-smell, of lilac and fresh tar.

At the centre of town I cut through the back of the parking lot behind the bank, crossed Main Street and continued on my way.

When the throughway underpass came into view, I saw the top halves of trucks rolling high up against the dark blue sky and, below them, framed by concrete walls and the slab of upper road, a darker and greener world: a beckoning world of winding roads and shuttered houses, a green blackness glimmering with yellow spots of street lamps, white spots of moonlight.

As I passed under the high, trembling roadbed on my way to the older part of town, the dark walls, spattered with chalked letters, made me think of hulking creatures risen from the underworld, bearing on their shoulders the lanes of a celestial bowling alley.

On the other side of the underpass I glanced up at the nearly full moon. It was a little blurred on one side, but so hard and sharp on the other that it looked as if I could cut my finger on it.

When I next looked up, the moon was partly blocked by black-green oak leaves. I was walking under high trees beside neck-high hedges. A mailbox on a post looked like a loaf of bread. Shafts of moonlight slanted down like boards.

I turned onto a darker street and after a while I stopped in front of a large house set back from the road.

And my idea, bred by the bold moon and the blue summer night, was suddenly clear to me: I would make my way around the house into the backyard, like a criminal. Maybe there would be a rope swing. Maybe she'd see me from an upper window. I had never visited her before, never walked home with her. What I felt was too hidden for that, too lost in dark, twisting tunnels. We were school friends, but our friendship had never stretched beyond the edges of school. Maybe I could leave some sign for her, something to show her that I'd come through the summer night, into her backyard.

I passed under one of the big tulip trees in the front yard and began walking along the side of the house. In a black window-pane I saw my sudden face. Somewhere I seemed to hear voices and when I stepped around the back of the house into the full radiance of the moon, I saw four girls playing ball.

They were playing Wiffle ball in the brilliant moonlight, as though it were a summer's day. Sonja was batting. I knew the three other girls, all of them in my classes: Marcia, pitching; Jeanie, taking a lead off first; Bernice, in the outfield, a few steps away from me. In the moonlight they were wearing clothes I'd never seen before, dungarees and shorts and sweat-shirts and boys' shirts, as if they were dressed up in a play about boys.

Bernice had on a baseball cap and wore a jacket tied around her waist. In school they wore knee-length skirts and neatly ironed blouses, light summer dresses with leather belts. The girl-boys excited and disturbed me, as if I'd stumbled into some secret rite. Sonja, seeing me, burst out laughing. 'Well look who's here,' she said, in the slightly mocking tone that kept me wary and always joking. 'Who is that tall stranger?' She stood holding the yellow Wiffle-ball bat on her shoulder, refusing to be surprised. 'Come on, don't just stand there, you can catch.' She was wearing dungarees rolled half-way up her calves, a floppy sweat-shirt with the sleeves pushed up above the elbows, low white sneakers without socks. Her hair startled me: it was pulled back to show her ears. I remembered the hair falling brown-blond along one side of her face.

They all turned to me now, smiled and waved me towards them, and with a sharp little laugh I sauntered in, pushing back my hair with my fingers, thrusting my hands deep into my dungaree pockets.

Then I was standing behind home plate, catching, calling balls and strikes. The girls took their game seriously, Sonja and Jeanie against Marcia and Bernice. Marcia had a sharp-breaking curveball that kept catching the corner of the upside-down pie tin. 'Strike?' yelled Sonja. 'My foot. It missed by a mile. Kill the umpire!' The flattened-back tops of her ears irritated me. Jeanie stood glaring at me, fists on hips. She wore an oversized boy's shirt longer than her shorts, so that she looked naked, as if she'd thrown a shirt over a pair of underpants – her tanned legs gleamed in the moonlight, her blond pony-tail bounced furiously with her slightest motion, and in the folds of her loose shirt her jumpy breasts, appearing and disappearing, made me think of balls of yarn. The girls swung hard, slid into paper-plate bases, threw like boys. They shouted 'Hey hey!' and 'Way to go!' After a while they let me play, each taking a turn at being umpire. As we played, it seemed to me that the girls were becoming unravelled: Marcia's lumberjack shirt was only partly tucked into her faded dungarees, wriggles of hair fell down along Jeanie's damp cheeks, Bernice, her braces glinting, flung off the jacket tied around her waist, one of Sonja's cuffs kept falling down. Marcia scooped up a grounder, whirled and threw to me at second, Sonja was racing from first, suddenly she slid – and sitting there on the grass below me, leaning back on her elbows, her legs stretched out on both sides of my feet, a copper rivet gleaming on the pocket of her dungarees, a bit of zipper showing, a hank of hair hanging over one eyebrow, she glared up at me, cried 'Safe by a mile!' and broke into wild laughter. Then Jeanie began to laugh, Marcia and Bernice burst out laughing, I felt something give way in my chest and I erupted in loud, releasing laughter, the laughter of childhood, until my ribs hurt and tears burned in my eyes – and again whoops and bursts of laughter, under the blue sky of the summer night.

Sonja stood up, pushed a fallen sleeve of her sweat-shirt above her elbow, and said, 'How about a Coke? I've about had it.' She wiped her tanned forearm across her damp forehead. We all followed her up the back steps into the moonlit kitchen. 'Keep it down, guys,' she whispered, raising her eyes to the ceiling, as she filled glasses with ice cubes, poured hissing, clinking sodas. The other girls went back outside with their glasses, where I could hear them talking through the open kitchen window. Sonja pushed herself up onto the counter next to the dishrack and I stood across from her, leaning back against the refrigerator.

I wanted to ask her whether they always played ball at night, or whether it was something that had happened only on this night, this dream-blue night, night of adventures and revelations – night of the impossible visit she hadn't asked me about. I wanted to hear her say that the blue night was the colour of old puzzle boxes, that the world was a blue mystery, that lying awake in bed she'd imagined me coming through the night to her backyard, but she only sat on the counter, swinging her legs, drinking her soda, saying nothing.

A broken bar of moonlight lay across the dishrack, fell sharply along a door below the counter, bent half-way along the linoleum before stopping in shadow.

She sat across from me with her hands on the silver strip at the edge of the counter, swinging her legs in and out of moonlight. Her knees were pressed together, but her calves were parted and one foot was half-turned towards the other. I could see her anklebones. Her dungarees were rolled into thick cuffs half-way up the calf, one slightly higher than the other. As her calves swung back against the counter, they became wider for a moment, before they swung out. The gentle swinging, the widening and narrowing calves, the rolled-up cuffs, the rubbery ribs of the dishrack, the glimmer of window above the mesh of the screen, all this seemed to me as mysterious as the summer moonlight, which had driven me through the night to this kitchen, where it glittered on knives and forks sticking out of the silverware box at the end of the dishrack and on her calves, swinging back and forth.

Now and then Sonja picked up her glass and, leaning back her head, took a rattling drink of soda. I could see the column of her throat moving as she swallowed and it seemed to me that although she was only sitting there, she was moving all over: her legs swung back and forth, her throat moved, her hands moved from the counter to the glass and back, and something seemed to come quivering up out of her, as if she'd swallowed a piece of burning-cool moonlight and were releasing it through her legs and fingertips.

Through the window screen I could see the moonlit grass of the backyard, the yellow plastic bat on the grass, a corner of shingled garage and a piece of purplish-blue night, and I could hear Marcia talking quietly, the faint rumble of trucks rolling through the sky, a sharp, clicking insect.

I felt bound in the dark blue spell of the kitchen, of the calves swinging back and forth, the glittering silverware, moonlight on linoleum, silence that seemed to be filling up with something like a stretching skin, somewhere a quivering, and I standing still, in the spell of it all, watchful. Her hands gripped the edge of the counter. Her calves moved back and forth under pressed-together knees. She was leaning forward at the waist, her eyes shone like black moonlight, there was a tension in her arms that I could feel in my own arms, a tension that rippled up into her throat, and suddenly she burst out laughing.

'What are you laughing at?' I said, startled, disappointed.

'Oh, nothing,' she said, slipping down from the counter. 'Everything. You, for example.' She walked over to the screen door. 'Let's call it a night, gang,' she said, opening the door. The three girls were sitting on the steps.

Marcia, taking a deep breath, slowly stretched out her arms and arched her back; and as her lumberjack shirt flattened against her, she seemed to be lifting her breasts towards the blue night sky, the summer moon.

Then there were quick good-nights and all three were walking across the lawn, turning out of sight behind the garage.

'This way, my good man,' Sonja said. Frowning, and putting a finger over her lips, she led me from the kitchen through the shadowy living-room, where I caught bronze and glass gleams – the edge of the fire shovel, a lamp base, the black glass of the television screen. At the front door flanked by thin strips of glass she turned the knob and opened the wooden door, held open the screen door. Behind her a flight of carpeted stairs rose into darkness. 'Fair Knight,' she said, with a little mock curtsy, 'farewell,' and pushed me out the door. I saw her arm rise and felt her fingers touch my face. With a laugh she shut the door.

It had happened so quickly that I wasn't sure what it was that had happened. Somewhere between 'farewell' and laughter a different thing had happened, an event from a higher, more hidden realm, something connected with the dark blue kitchen, the glittering silverware and swinging legs, the mystery of the blue summer night. It was as if, under the drifting-down light of the moon, under the white-blue light that kept soaking into things, dissolving the day-world, a new shape had been released.

I stood for a while in front of the darkened front door, as if waiting for it to turn into something else – a forest path, a fluttering curtain. Then I walked away from the house along red-black slabs of slate, looked back once over my shoulder at the dark windows, and turned onto the sidewalk under high oaks and elms.

I felt a new lightness in my chest, as if an impediment to breathing had been removed. It was a night of revelations, but I now saw that each particle of the night was equal to the others. The moonlit path of black notes on the page of the music book, the yellow bat lying on just those blades of grass, the precise tilt of each knife in the dishrack, Sonja's calves swinging in and out of moonlight, Marcia's slowly arching back, the hand rising towards my face, all this was as unique and unrepeatable as the history of an ancient kingdom. For I had wanted to take a little walk before going to bed, but I had stepped from my room into the first summer night, the only summer night.

Under the high trees the moonlight fell steadily. I could see it sifting down through the leaves. All night long it had fallen into backyards, on chimneys and stop signs, on the cross-pieces of telephone poles and on sidewalks buckled by tree roots. Down through the leaves it was slowly sifting, sticking to the warm air, forming clumps in the leaf-shadows. I could feel the moonlight lying on my hands. A weariness came over me, a weariness trembling with exhilaration. I had the sensation that I was expanding, growing lighter. Under the branches the air was becoming denser with moonlight, I could scarcely push my way through. My feet seemed to be pressing down on thick, spongy air. I felt an odd buoyancy, and when I looked down I saw that I was walking a little above the sidewalk. I raised my foot and stepped higher. Then I began to climb the thick tangle of moonlight and shadow, slipping now and then, sinking a little, pulling myself up with the aid of branches, and soon I came out over the top of a tree into the clearness of the moon. Dark fields of blue air stretched away in every direction. I looked down at the moonlit leaves below, at the top of a street lamp, at shafts of moonlight slanting like white ladders under the leaves. I walked carefully forward above the trees, taking light steps that sank deep, then climbed a little higher, till catching a breeze I felt myself borne away into the blue countries of the night.

The dream of the consortium

The purchase of the department store by the consortium filled us with uneasiness and secret hope. The department store was the last of the grand old emporiums in our city; from earliest childhood we had ridden its ageing escalators and wandered its faded departments. Our very idea of excess, of wonder, had been formed by its shelves of merchandise stretching into brown distances and rising through all twelve floors. In the glare of the new glass mall the old stores had vanished one by one, already our visits to the fading department store had become tinged with resignation and melancholy. Therefore the purchase of the department store by the consortium was a sharp blow, even a devastation, but at the same time a solace, for hadn't we always known that our store was nothing but an awkward survivor, almost an embarrassment, in a certain sense an illusion?

From the very first it was said that the consortium planned to preserve the block-long building down to the last architectural detail, from the ornamental leaves and berries on its entrance columns to the quaint nineteenth-century marble fountain located in a far corner of the ground floor. It was rumoured that the preserved building was to be turned into suites of offices, but immediately a counter-rumour arose and now it was whispered that the consortium planned to revive the department store, to restore it to its former grandeur. Reports began to circulate that the consortium had been purchasing other department stores in other cities, that factories and warehouses belonging to the consortium were springing up in remote places. To all such talk we listened with a certain reserve, for we no longer knew whether we really desired the rebirth of our department store or longed only for its continuance in a perpetual brown twilight of decline.

The opening was to take place in early spring. All that fall and winter we waited anxiously, while behind the large display windows, covered by white sheets, we heard the sounds of workmen's radios, of banging and sawing, of heavy loads scraping across floors; and high above, in the white skies of winter, the dark scaffolding seemed a complex, riddling work of destruction.

We thought, without speaking of it, of long-drawn-out childhood waiting, of the waiting that gradually becomes infected with anxiety, with unhappiness, as the dreamed-of day, drawing closer and closer, grows heavy with the burden of impossible desires.

And the day came, a day like all others, a cool bright mid-April morning. And we were struck by surprise: before our eyes, but as if secretly, a grand department store had sprung up, a new emporium that seemed always to have been there, obscured by the shadow of our faded hopes. The new store rose nineteen storeys into the bright blue day. In the broad plate-glass windows of the ground floor and the brilliant, arched windows of the renovated granite façade, distorted reflections of red and brown office buildings seemed to tremble and shimmer.

Despite the already opening doors it was impossible not to pause at the display windows, for the consortium, as if sensing our hesitation, had spared no expense in its effort to hold us there. One window showed a sandy beach with a tide line of seaweed and shells, and a strip of ocean with low waves breaking. The brilliantly realistic scene, with its bright blue sky and slow-drifting blue-shadowed clouds, its mannequin life-guard on his white chair, its low waves breaking and scraping back, breaking and scraping back, its distant lighthouse no larger than a thimble, was inhabited in the foreground by three slender mannequin women sunning themselves in shiny silver bathing suits. Suddenly they sat up, revealing to spectators that they were real women pretending to be mannequins – and suddenly they lay down rigidly, making us wonder whether they were automated mannequins pretending to be real women; and the lifeguard refused to move, refused to give a sign; while seagulls that might have been real or might have been ingenious models strutted about in the sand.

We smiled, we frowned thoughtfully, we granted the windows a certain originality, but at the same time we held back, we resisted the temptation to be captivated. After all, it wasn't such shows we longed for, but something else entirely, something that carried us back to better times, when we still had hope, something to be found only on the inside. Is it a wonder we hesitated?

Slowly, a little nervously, we made our way through the great arch of the renovated entranceway, towards a row of new glass doors. Panes of glass slid silently apart at our approach and ushered us towards an inner row of antique revolving doors, slow and dark, which reminded us of our childhood and of old black-and-white movies, and led into the store itself.

We found ourselves in an immense Grand Court that rose to the height of three floors. A broad aisle lined with mannequins dressed in bustles and petticoats, top hats and greatcoats, led to the restored fountain with its six sculptures representing Honesty, Industry, Invention, Commerce, Thrift and The Republic. And we were pleased, we were pleased: our fountain had never looked so splendid. But we were no fools, we understood perfectly that this evocation of a vanished golden age, an age in which none of us entirely believed, was a calculated appeal to something dubious in our natures. And yet we admired the shrewdness of the appeal, even as we refused to be taken in by it. We saw at once that the deliberately outmoded architectural style was mixed with aggressively modern touches, such as the glass elevators that rose along openwork steel columns, and the grand stairway, composed not of marble but of elegant curving escalators with transparent sides that led to a mezzanine where customers were already drinking coffee at white metal tables that gave a view of the Grand Court below. The bold clash of the old-fashioned and the ultramodern, each setting off the other, each designed to flatter us, to disarm our scepticism, was the most striking effect achieved by the consortium, whose deeper innovations and intentions revealed themselves gradually.

With such thoughts we ascended the escalators and the glass elevators, we moved warily into the departments, felt our way farther into the depths of the store.

We who have grown up with the old department stores know that one of their secret pleasures is the sudden, violent transitions between departments, the startling juxtapositions, as in the kind of museum where a room full of old fire engines opens into a hall lined with glass cases containing owls, herons and sandpipers. In the new department store we saw the art of juxtaposition raised to bold and unexpected heights. With the exception of the Grand Court, which maintained the straight lines of the classical store, the departments of every floor had been designed to emerge suddenly and dramatically one from the other. So great an effort had been made by the interior designers to avoid clear vistas that many of the aisles were elaborately curved. From a shadowy, meandering pathway of highboys, glass-fronted bookcases and rolltop desks with pigeonholes, there burst into view a bright unsettling place of long-legged mannequins with pink and green hair, wearing flashes of black satin and white lace. Here and there on glass counters, like mutilated corpses in a mad killer's basement, rose the lower halves of female bodies, upside down with legs in the air – and as we made our way towards pairs of inverted legs in shiny black stockings studded with tiny green jewels, suddenly we found ourselves wandering among frostless refrigerators, three-tier dishwashers, microwave ovens with digital displays. A bored-looking mannequin with short black hair, who seemed to have strayed from her department, leaned against a refrigerator and revealed the latest brassiere from Italy, consisting of a single gold thread that crossed her breasts in a straight line and fastened with a heart-shaped clasp in back. Such transitions and confusions seemed to invite us to lose our way, despite the glass-covered maps posted everywhere; and we who wanted nothing better than to lose our way plunged deeper into the winding aisles, grateful for anything that increased our sense of the store's abundance, that satisfied our secret longing for an endless multiplication of departments.

This quality of surprise, this continual attempt to banish monotony and elude a sense of constriction, was also evident in one of the consortium's more pleasing innovations. From time to time at the ends of turning aisles we came to broad, open areas where shoppers overcome by fatigue might rest before continuing on their way. Each area, designated as a plaza on the store maps, was designed in a distinct style. The floor of one such plaza was composed of real earth and grass. In the centre rose a large oak tree with spreading branches, hung with Chinese lanterns, beneath which stood a scattering of slatted wooden benches. Another plaza was in the style of a foggy London street at night; clouds of yellowish fog were pumped in by a fog machine, obscuring the lamp-posts and the mannequin bobby with his polished billy club. And on an upper floor we discovered a Victorian parlour, where we sank down in the plump armchairs, under the gas lighting-fixtures, among the oval photographs, the whatnots, the marble statues.

The artful plazas alone might have assured the success of the opening day, for already there were those among us who were eager to search all nineteen floors for plazas in period designs, but other innovations also attracted our attention. We were struck by the variety of accessory services and entertainments, located mainly on the four underground levels but also among the upper floors, such as the replicated shoeshine parlour, the old barber shop with its striped pole turning in a column of glass, the general store with its barrels of penny candy, the kinetoscope parlour on the eighth floor, the basement vaudeville theatre with its four daily performances. We noted the many coffee shops, restaurants and luncheonettes in scrupulously reproduced styles: the Pullman dining car, the eighteenth-century New England inn, the whaling ship, the pueblo village, the frontier saloon with swinging doors. And we discovered on each floor, as we emerged from a maze of meandering departments, sudden places the purpose of which appeared to be cultural or educational, although we sensed that their real intention was to interrupt the inevitable boredom of displayed merchandise with refreshing surprises – surprises that permitted the customer to return with renewed vigour to the strenuous adventure of buying. Thus the consortium had provided for our instruction a mannequin manufactory, with a bearded sculptor at work on a clay figure before a live model, in a setting of plaster casts, discarded hands and feet, and nearly finished fibreglass figures to which an assistant was adding glass eyes, wigs and teeth; a meticulous replication of four galleries chosen from the Prado, the Uffizi, the Rijksmuseum and the Hermitage, with expert reproductions of all the paintings, frames and statues, and three uniformed guides who explained to small groups of shoppers the history and technique of each work of art; and a reproduced portion of Egyptian pyramid with steps leading down to two burial chambers and a mortuary temple.

Perhaps because of the size of the new department store, the large number of plazas and cultural areas, the services and entertainments, the sheer assault on our nervous systems of nineteen floors and four basement levels of merchandise, we didn't at first take special note of the new departments scattered throughout the store in what we took to be a spirit of whimsy, of exuberant invention. Such was the department of streams, pools and waterfalls, located in a suddenly appearing alcove of the landscaping department, or, on the fourteenth floor, between men's hats and notions, the gloomy department of caves and tunnels, where dim fluorescent bulbs set in the cave walls shed a purplish glow over the rock formations, and price tags hung from neatly labelled stalactites, flowstone, cave coral, twisting helictites. One of the more mysterious departments lay beyond a soft brown world of night tables, dimly glowing lamps, pulled-back bedspreads displaying flowery sheets, and four-poster beds with arched canopies and heavy curtains. At the end of a narrow path of bunkbeds filled with tigers and elephants, there suddenly appeared a high, whitish area that seemed to be under construction. Here and there on the floor stood broken marble columns and blocks of cracked stone, against one wall was a flight of crumbling steps leading nowhere, at a shiny wooden counter in one corner sat a man in a grey suit and maroon tie who seemed to await us.

It was generally conceded that opening day had been a striking success. Oh, there were doubters among us, doubters who felt that the whole thing should be torn down and forgotten, but on the whole we were inclined to be hopeful. To begin with, it was clear to us that the consortium had created a serious rival to the mall. And in a move obviously intended to broaden the eroding customer base of the traditional department store, the new emporium directly challenged the deluxe speciality store by offering, in addition to its abundance of moderately priced goods, a wide range of high-priced speciality items, from sequinned evening gowns and chauffeur's livery to jewelled chess sets and imported jade palace dogs from the Imperial Palace of Beijing. We were attracted by the Grand Court and the renovated fountain, by the meandering aisles, by the clever replications, by the brashness and energy of the whole enterprise; and if we were inclined to reserve judgement, to withhold our approval, at the same time we were prepared to return.

We returned with the sharp sense that we had barely begun to explore the store, that further explorations were in fact necessary if we were to penetrate its still elusive nature. Within days we noticed that the store was already changing. Aisles here and there had been shifted slightly to make room for new merchandise, departments that we did not recall seeing had sprung up or were about to open, it was said that plans were already under way for a penthouse and a floor beneath the four basement levels; and in what was either a restless desire for expansion or a calculated effort to avoid tedium, small changes had been introduced in the design of individual departments.

But it was above all the unusual departments, which we hadn't observed closely on opening day, that now drew our deepest attention. It quickly became evident that these were not witty or bizarre architectural elements designed to raise smiles of appreciation or frowns of curiosity, but were serious departments in their own right, intent on sales. By the end of the first week the department of streams, pools and waterfalls had begun doing a brisk business, mostly from suburban customers with large properties who were able to select from a wide range of meticulously distinguished styles: twelve models of brook or stream alone were on display, from the shallow rocky straight

bed to the deep sandy winding bed. The caves and tunnels of
the fourteenth floor were intended not only for privately owned
hills and slopes but also for cellars, attics and playrooms. We
returned to the high, whitish place that had appeared to be
under construction, only to discover our error. In a thick
catalogue fastened to the counter by a chain, the sales clerk
pointed to an array of ruins: all the architectural orders were
being offered for sale, including carefully differentiated Greek
Doric and Roman Doric, as well as three varieties of Corinthian
capital, reproduced either in the original stone or, less expen-
sively, in a synthetic equivalent, and in various stages of ruin.
For this was the department of classical ruins, from which one
could also purchase friezes, broken pediments, crumbling
arches, picturesque fragments of temples and mausoleums. At
the back of the book were photographs of the Parthenon, the
Colosseum, a Roman aqueduct, all in lush garden settings.
Patiently the sales clerk answered our sceptical, ardent questions. Everything in the catalogue could be ordered; all parts
were manufactured in repro factories and shipped direct. Only
the other day a Texas oilman had ordered the Colosseum for his
ranch. The majority of orders came from corporations looking
for innovative ideas in the landscaping line; a software company in New Mexico had recently ordered the Baths of Caracalla
and Hadrian's Villa for its ten-acre business park, and another
firm in southern California had ordered the entire Acropolis,
sturdier than the original and guaranteed against pollution, set
by the shore of an ornamental lake. The average customer was
of course more likely to want a ruined column for the hall or
backyard.

We shook our heads, we grew thoughtful, we began to smile
but felt the edges of our smiles crumbling; and as we entered
more familiar departments, making our way through squash
rackets, lacrosse sticks and ping-pong tables, past TV/VCR
stands, audio-visual cabinets and stereo-rack systems with five-

band graphic equalizers, past cookie jars shaped like smiling raccoons and umbrellas with wooden handles shaped like ducks, our sense of something odd and inexplicable about the new departments, something in the manner of a violation, gave way gradually to the conviction that it was our own perception which was at fault. Far from being alien intrusions into a familiar world, the new departments were nothing but an extension of that world. For wasn't it in the nature of department stores to offer for sale everything under the sun? Wasn't the secret premise of such places that the whole world was a bazaar? The consortium, in a bold leap designed to counter the power of the mall, had simply extended the boundaries of the buyable. Nor was the idea of imitation or replication in the slightest degree alien in this world of synthetic materials and expensive reproductions of old-fashioned toys, famous paintings and period furniture.

Yet even then, in those early days of excitement and discovery, we failed to grasp the startling boldness of the new managers, despite hints and glimpses that left us a little breathless.

It was precisely in those days, as we were feeling our way into the new store, that a harsh campaign was waged against it, originating from interests serving the speciality shops and the mall. The new store, it was charged, was poorly designed, filled with wasted space and concerned more with atmosphere than with the efficient display of merchandise; the relationship of departments was confusing; the flashy new departments, by their very nature, could appeal to only a small number of customers; the plazas were tasteless, the architecture grotesque, the attractions absurd. Such easily refuted charges were no more than the familiar stuff of business rivalry, but concerns were voiced by ordinary citizens as well. Some argued that the store, despite its smattering of innovations, represented a return to the past; they accused the consortium of trading shamelessly on our nostalgia, and pointed in particular to the emphasis on imitation and replication in the designs of the plazas and cultural areas and even in the merchandise itself. Others, acknowledging the attractiveness and success of the new venture, argued that the very completeness of that success was disturbing, since customers were often reluctant to tear themselves away from the delights of the renovated emporium and complained of a feeling of disappointment or irritation when they stepped back into the street.

Perhaps inspired by these attacks, perhaps prompted by our own doubts and desires, we set out in the course of the next few weeks to explore the new store in detail, to burrow into its depths, to permit none of its elements to escape our interrogation.

Above the thirteenth floor, old-fashioned wood-panelled elevators with brass fittings, operated by polite young men in dark red jackets and black pants, rose through the remaining six floors. And on every level, at two widely separated places, elegant escalators trimmed in mahogany and brass rose up, while beside them, at an angle forming an X, stairfuls of customers floated to the floors below.

We passed among dinner plates with pictures of blue windmills on them, footed glass dessert dishes filled with wax apricots, brightly coloured ten-cup coffeemakers with built-in digital clocks. We wandered past glittering arrays of laser printers and laptops, past brightly painted circus wagons, rolls of brown canvas and bales of hay, through mazes of pale green bathtubs, onyx sinks set in oak cabinets, pink water closets carved with cherubs. In the depths of the toy department, which covered most of the eleventh and twelfth floors, there was a sub-department that sold full-sized Ferris wheels, merry-go-rounds and roller-coasters. Nearby we discovered an alcove of scale-model cities, including precise wooden and plaster models of Victorian London, Nuremberg in the age of Dürer and Manhattan in 1925, each containing more than sixty thousand separate pieces and capable of being assembled in a frame the size of a sandbox. In the bargain basement on the second underground level there were alcoves and sub-departments selling imperfect mannequins, discarded display-window props, and selected marked-down items from the more popular plazas and restaurants: trompe-l'oeil vistas painted on cardboard, cobblestones made of fibreglass, papier-mâché bricks. New departments appeared to be springing up everywhere, as if to keep pace with our desires; and it was rumoured that somewhere on the fourteenth or fifteenth floor, in a small department with a desk and a catalogue, corporations with fabulous sums at their disposal could order full-sized replicas of entire ancient cities.

Such rumours lent excitement to our investigations, but at the same time they obscured our sense of things, they contaminated our perceptions, so that among us there arose a new scepticism, which itself interfered with the direct evidence of our senses and delayed for a while our deeper understanding of the store.

In the meantime all but the harshest among us had begun to succumb to the new window displays, which were being carried to heights of daring and ingenuity unknown to us before. We heard that the consortium had hired from a grey, ice-bound city in eastern or northern Europe, where the pale sun shone for only two hours a day, a brooding and temperamental window-display artist, providing him with a staff of mannequin makers, automaton masters, miniaturists, stage-set designers and window engineers, and promising him an unheard-of freedom in developing the display windows of the new store. Every day one of the many plate-glass windows on all four sides of the block-long building was covered with a red velvet curtain, which rose the following morning on a brand-new display. One window showed a six-foot scale model of a thirty-four-storey hotel, in which each of its more than two hundred rooms was lit up in turn, revealing in each instance an exquisitely detailed scene performed by miniature automated figures: a little man was murdering a little woman with repeated stabbings of a little bloody knife, a beautiful miniature lady seated at a vanity table with an ornate mirror was reading a letter and weeping hysterically, a young woman opened a closet and was embraced by a skeleton. In another display window, full-sized mobile mannequins in jewelled sunglasses and transparent silk bathing suits assumed elegant, languorous poses in a realistic jungle setting populated by live parrots and monkeys, as well as a disturbing lion that paced back and forth and only gradually revealed itself to be a machine. One of the more popular windows was a marionette theatre, in which plays with diverse settings – a Mississippi paddle steamer, a Turkish harem, a Parisian fashion show stalked by a strangler – were performed by marionettes whose costumes had been designed by a celebrated couturier and whose coiffures were fashioned by their personal hair stylist. Despite such allusions to the sale of merchandise, many of the windows revelled in their freedom and quickly developed in purely artistic directions. A striking window of this kind began as a conventional display of animated mannequins in transparent raincoats and bikini underwear and grew swiftly into a series of variations on the theme of rain: a rain machine, a wind machine, mirrors and coloured lights combined to form shifting patterns of wind-swept rain, as if the display artist were engaged in the exploration of a new art, an art of rain. Yet even such windows, which seemed to disdain the vulgar sale of merchandise and aspire to higher things, tantalized us by their very aloofness and made us search for secret relations that continued to elude us.

It wasn't until the end of the third or fourth week, when the criticisms had diminished to a mere whisper, when even the doubters had to admit that the new store had about it an air of solidity and permanence, that we at last permitted ourselves to give way entirely to the lure of the new emporium, to abandon ourselves to the meandering aisles, the hidden alcoves. We applauded the adventurous window displays, welcomed the newest and most daring departments, wandered the floors delighting in every shift and change, in the always varied rhythms of the interior design. Departments of steel radial tyres, salted nuts, snow blowers, shower curtains printed with reproductions of famous Impressionist paintings (*Luncheon of the Boating Party*, *Camille Monet and Her Cousin on the Beach at Trouville*, *Impression: Sunrise*) and triple-track windows gave way to departments of Moorish courtyards, volcanoes, Aztec temples. These new and unconventional departments formed no pattern of distribution, but as we ascended escalators and strode through swiftly changing scenes, it came over us that the distinction between old and new, familiar and unfamiliar, was our own. The store itself made no such distinction, but simply offered its wide-ranging merchandise for sale. Was there really, after all, so great a difference between a wrist-watch and a Roman villa? In the new emporium, with its noble and feverish desire to surpass its rivals and recapture, in the last decade of the twentieth century, the vanished glory of the great department stores, you could purchase quartz heaters, power mowers, Venetian palazzi, electric pencil sharpeners, Scottish castles, cordless phones with ten-channel autoscan, flying buttresses, mulching tractors, Neolithic villages, aluminium siding, the palace of Sargon II, the Erie Canal, wax museums, submersible sump pumps, Sumerian ziggurats, islands with palm trees and crashing surf, ancient Troy, motorized wheelchairs, Viking burial mounds, the Great Mosque of Córdoba, lagoons, sphinxes, exercycles, black leather recliners, Upper Paleolithic caves with drawings of bison, three-ring circuses, the Colossus

of Rhodes, bo-tree shrines, Coca-Cola bottling plants, Muto-
scopes, zoom lenses, casbahs, African diamond mines, Benedic-
tine monasteries, ice-cream makers, the Library of Alexandria,
Zouave uniforms, opera theatres, five-speed drill presses, clavi-
cembali, film-noir stage sets, deserts with mirages, cotton gins,
hennins, steaming square miles of Amazon jungle, old piers
with seagulls.

In remote factories located in large underpopulated states,
teams of workers trained in secret workshops taught by rigorous
experts were producing replicas so skilful that the originals had
begun to seem a little flawed, a little faded and unconvincing.

It was said that in a department on the fifteenth or sixteenth
floor, near shades and drapes, in a small room resembling a
travel agency, with maps on the walls and two old desks heaped
with brochures, the heads of four major hotel chains, angered
by the scandalous loss of billions of dollars each year to foreign
countries through tourism, were discussing plans to purchase
the exact replication of a small European country, with its lakes
and mountains, its quaint villages with cobblestoned streets and
carved door panels, its railroads and postage stamps, for
placement in central Texas or western Montana. The hotel
executives believed that Americans would enjoy the conven-
ience of visiting Europe directly by car or bus; the pleasure of
the trip would be enhanced by the knowledge that, whenever
the traveller grew bored or lonely, as so often happened in
foreign countries, he could hop in his car and drive across the
simulated border into America itself.

The brashness of the plan filled us with a kind of nervous
exhilaration. Similar deals, we began to realize, were taking
place in departments on other floors. We imagined mountain
ranges of artificial snow, sparkling false lakes, replicated forests,
nightingales, thunderstorms. We dreamed of Florence rising
stone by stone from a desert in Arizona; we saw, in the depths of
China, the slow and meticulous reconstruction of New England,

with its sugar maples and old brick factories, its exact pattern of rooftops, stoplights, leaf-shade, riverbanks – and, on each riverbank, the precise shaft of sunlight slanting through pines onto a picnic table trembling with sun and shade.

There was no longer any need to verify such rumours and suspicions, for we sensed in ourselves a secret sympathy with the store, a profound intuition of its mysteries. The consortium was determined to satisfy the buyer's secret desire: to appropriate the world, to possess it entirely. Countless factories were turning out precise pieces of geography and history, multiplying them relentlessly. In some department half-hidden by shelves of merchandise, plans were no doubt under way for duplicating and selling still larger pieces of real estate: the Mediterranean shore with its famous beaches and resorts, the Black Sea, ancient Persia. If we wandered here long enough, we would find departments so audacious that to imagine them clearly would be to suffer harm, as from the blow of a hammer. With such visions and premonitions swirling within, we pressed to the utmost ends of the store, searching out unseen corners, feverishly ascending and descending a series of zigzag escalators, passing through departments we had seen so quickly that already they looked unfamiliar.

It was on one of these feverish journeys that we descended past the lowest of the subterranean levels to a new level still under construction. In a thick darkness lit here and there by greenish lights, tunnels braced with heavy posts stretched in every direction. Workers wearing helmets with lights in them raised their glistening arms to swing pickaxes against rockfaces. Even in this raw region of barely imagined departments, men in neat suits were measuring distances with metallic tape measures, marking the ground with chalk. A freestanding door lay against a rocky wall beside an opening, and a man in a necktie ushered us inside.

The department was almost black, lit by a reddish glow. Here and there men and women moved with strangely formal gestures, as if they were engaged in a mysterious dance. Women of intolerable beauty turned their faces towards us slowly, with sad smiles; we had the sensation of having entered some dark and melancholy dream. Only gradually did we realize that the figures were on display. The art of mobile holography, a salesman was saying, was on the verge of another breakthrough – these images, under carefully controlled conditions, were able to stimulate in the spectator a sensation of touch and to give the illusion of life itself. Slowly a demon-eyed woman glided towards us; as she came closer we felt, in our fingertips, a faint tingle or tickle. She continued to smile vaguely at us as we snatched away our hands.

We no longer resist it, we no longer try to resist it, the new emporium. These dangerous descents, these dubious wanderings, tug at us even in our sleep. New departments spring up almost daily, sales records are continually surpassed, from the receiving rooms comes an unbroken rumble of arriving goods. There is talk of four new upper storeys, of deeper excavations, of the purchase of a neighbouring commercial building that will be joined to the old building by three glassed-in bridges; such rumours, however false, strike us as essentially true. In this we are merely acknowledging the power of the new store, the thoroughness of its triumph. For as the departments multiply, as the store grows and invents itself daily, so it expands within our minds until everything else is pressed flat against our skulls. Indeed it is not always pleasant to leave the new emporium, and as we glance irritably at our watches we search for excuses to linger among the winding aisles and sudden alcoves, to delay our departure a little. But at last we must step through the parting glass doors, bewildered to find ourselves in sunlight; across from us the buildings, dark rose in hue, lie in late afternoon shadow. In the black plate-glass windows opposite we see the bright green-and-white reflection of a passing bus, through which a row of half-closed blinds is visible. Overhead, the avenue-wide strip of sky is brilliant blue. As we hurry along the sidewalk, we have the absurd sensation that we have entered still another department, composed of ingeniously lifelike streets with artful shadows and reflections – that our destinations lie in a far corner of the same department – that we are condemned to hurry forever through these artificial halls, bright with late afternoon light, in search of a way out.

Balloon flight, 1870

The Prussians surround us; there's no way out; and so I rise jerkily into the air, one hand gripping the waist-high side of the swaying wicker basket, the other gripping one of the cords rising from the basket to the hoop above, while down below I see the upturned faces, the upstretched arms, the waving hats and kepis, I hear cries of Vive la France! and Vive la République! in the windy blue October air. Vallard, my pilot, stands beside me in his tight-wrapped greatcoat as calmly as though he were looking in the window of a pork butcher's shop. My mission is simple: to fly over the Prussian lines, to land in unoccupied France, to organize resistance in the provinces. Later I will join Gambetta in Tours. The dangers are many; the destination uncertain as the wind; but now in the late morning sunlight, as I rise over the rooftops of Paris, I'm taken by the grand spectacle below, by the shining gilt dome of the Invalides, the uneven towers of Saint-Sulpice, the rows of big-wheeled bronze cannon in the Tuileries gardens, flocks of sheep in the city squares, soldiers bathing in the Seine beside a blown-up bridge, and look! the semaphore station on top of the Arc de Triomphe, the river like a green crescent moon bending through the city, people on rooftops looking out towards the forts and hills. And on every street a tremor of light and colour, National Guards in their red kepis and blue tunics and red trousers, ladies' parasols yellow and violet and green, the glint of long bayonets at the ends of rifles, and there the red turban of a Zouave, over there a sudden flash of brass – a cavalry officer's helmet with its mane of horsehair – as we drift in a south-east wind towards the north-western ramparts.

———

The thick, crenellated wall that surrounds Paris is thirty feet high, with ninety-four projecting bastions. The wall is riddled with gun slits and supplied with heavy cannon. National Guards, army regulars, and Mobiles from the provinces stand guard day and night at the top of the wall. Paris, city of light, city of twenty thousand cafés, has become a medieval fortress. Beyond the wall is a moat ten feet wide. Beyond the moat is a circle of sixteen forts, each with fifty to seventy heavy guns. In the hills beyond the perimeter of forts lie the siege lines of Moltke's armies. Was ever a city so well defended? Paris is impregnable. We will never surrender.

———

Below us I can see soldiers looking up from the top of the wall. They wave their kepis, raise their rifle butts in salute. Just outside the western ramparts, on the Butte Mortemart in the Bois de Boulogne, I see an orange flash of fire, smoke like chimney-smoke turned sideways. The smoke sits on the air like snow on a wall. I can make out the red of the gunners' caps. Barouches and landaus press close to the great gun, women in long-trained dresses stand watching, for the firing of the heavy guns has become one of the amusements of Paris.

Above me swells the great yellow balloon, made of varnished cotton and filled with coal gas. It is fifty feet wide – a fine target for a Prussian needle-gun. A single bullet piercing the cloth will turn the heavens into a ball of deadly flame. But the immediate danger, as we drift between the northern and western forts, is from the unpredictable motions of the balloon itself. Vallard can make it rise by casting off bags of sand, he can make it descend by pulling the valve rope and releasing gas, but even he cannot control the sudden shifts of wind, the swing and lurch of the basket, the temperature of the air, which causes the gas to expand and contract. Vallard studies the mariner's compass that hangs on a rope from the hoop above, reads the barometer that swings beside it. Both of us well know that a balloon is unsteerable. Inventors have proposed sails, propellers, fleets of birds straight out of fable. If only the sides of the basket came higher! The hills, russet with autumn, conceal Prussian gun batteries. In the chill clear air I hear the sudden sharp cry of a cock, from some unknown farmyard.

I cling to a cord, steady myself against the low basket-edge, and look down at fields and copses, scattered farms, a village with a church. Vallard tells me we're at one thousand feet. It is almost peaceful now, in the brisk October air. Hills red and brown, patches of yellow, the rippling shadow of our balloon. Up here you might almost forget the Prussian encampments in the woods, the sandbags in the windows of the Louvre, the dinners of horsemeat, the faces of the deserters fleeing into Montparnasse from the battle of Châtillon, the beds for wounded soldiers in the greenroom of the Comédie-Française, here in the

sky, the calm blue sky, as we drift over the autumn woods, the
sunny peaceful fields.

––––––

Suddenly, from out of a cluster of trees, an Uhlan appears on a
black horse. His gleaming helmet with its high crest is like the
dome of some exotic church. I can see the sabre hanging by his
leg, the white sash slashing his chest. As he looks up at our
balloon, a second Uhlan emerges from the copse, gazing up at
us, holding in one hand an upright lance taller than his horse. A
pennon flutters at the top of the lance. Now they begin to
pursue us; they shout; I see a third Uhlan, a fourth. I hear the
sharp report of a rifle. A flock of crows rises screaming from the
trees. Vallard cuts the cord of a sandbag hanging over the side of
the basket, cuts a second, a third; we rush upwards; the basket
sways dangerously; something stings my hand; a streak of
blood; the Uhlans are far below, eight of them, ten; I wrap
my bullet-grazed hand. The Uhlans, growing smaller and
smaller, ride after us as we ascend swaying into the cold regions
of upper air.

––––––

We have ascended to an elevation of ten thousand feet and in
the bright cold air I look down at a world I no longer recognize:
irregular patches of green and violet-brown, winding dark lines
like scratches, bits of cloud like floating snow. Here, at this
height, where men are invisible, where there is only Nature, one
is shaken, disturbed. I think of the vastness of Nature and the
littleness of Man, but my thought is inexact, it fails to express
the feeling that moves in me like a darkness. It's as if within me
a rift has opened; a fissure; a wound; yes; not the bullet's
scratch, but an inner crack; and there in that blackness, all's
without meaning; whether I strive or sleep; yawn or bleed;

accomplish my mission or drift to the moon; and in that ugly blackness, there's no difference between Paris and Berlin; between Paris and pissing. Hateful heights! Here there is only the death of dreams, dark laughter of fallen angels with hellfire wings. A terrible indifference courses through me, shakes me to the core. And always a little voice that whispers, whispers: what does it matter, this thing or that thing ... I look at my cold hand, clinging to the basket's rim. Fingers, I say, fingers, fingers, but I cannot understand the word. People have hands. Hands have fingers. There are five fingers on each hand. There are ten fingers on both hands. France is a nation. England is a nation of shopkeepers. Clovis, King of the Frankish nation, defeated the Roman legions at Soissons. Gaius Julius Caesar was assassinated in 44 BC. I see an icicle on Vallard's moustache.

———

It has passed like a dizziness, like a madness, even as Vallard pulls the valve rope and we begin to descend from those perilous regions. I look at Vallard, a man of few words, stolid, unchanged. A broad-shouldered man of twenty-six, the son of peasants from a village near Rouen. He has assured me that the provinces will rise and crush the invader. Vallard tells the story of a peasant who, coming upon a Prussian patrol, fell on him and tore out his throat with his teeth. I ask him where he learned to pilot a balloon. 'Gare d'Orléans,' he says in his laconic fashion, and at once I see the great waiting room of the Gare d'Orléans, the long workbenches where rows of seam-stresses sit stitching together large strips of calico in the light of gas lamps, the sailors braiding rope and fashioning the netting that encloses the balloons, workers in blue blouses assembling a wicker basket. On the floor of the great room, beside the abandoned railway tracks, partially inflated balloons, enormous and sagging, lie stretched out on their sides, their great curves looming over the workers and reaching half-way up the height of the walls. High overhead, from the station girders under the glass-and-iron roof, a few wicker baskets hang from ropes. It is in one of these training baskets that Vallard prepared for our flight, as he looked down at the long workbenches, the rows of gas lamps in the walls, the women's hands stitching, the valves of the great balloons lying across the tracks.

———

Where to look? Not down, for still I see an unpeopled world, a world without meaning, and like the tearing of a ligament the rift begins to open, the inner wound begins to bleed. Not up, for above me I see the bottom of a yellow monster carrying me off in its claws to hellish heaven. Straight ahead then? No, for before me lie vast stretches of unearthly blue – sinister blue – a nausea of blue. I do not fear death. I am prepared to die for France. But I fear this blue nothingness, this little voice that whispers, whispers: O what does it matter, this thing or that thing, Paris or Prussia, breath-warm or corpse-cold. And a loathing comes over me, for all the world of upper air, this mocking blue heaven with its little black secret. Sick to death of it all, I fix my gaze on the humble basket: on the strands of wicker woven by rough hands, on the six-fluked anchor dangling over the side, on the leather sacks containing government dispatches and ten thousand private letters, on the bags of ballast, the coil of rope, the basket of pigeons that will be used by provincials to send messages back to Paris. The wicker. The leather. The iron. The rope. I am calm now.

———

Moltke's investing troops are spread out in an indefensible perimeter of fifty miles. They hope to starve us into submission, but we will never surrender. Today we eat horsemeat and butter our bread with yellow horsefat. And tomorrow? Tomorrow we'll dine on paving stones! But we must act. The thought of our idleness fills me with rage. The First and Second German Armies are pinned down in Lorraine before the walls of Metz, but if Metz should fall? What then? Two armies would be released to reinforce the lines of investment about Paris, or to engage Gambetta in the south. We must attack! A double advance cannot possibly fail: a sortie *en masse* from the gates of Paris and a simultaneous attack behind the German lines. Gambetta, fretting at Tours, is eager to recapture Orléans and march north to Paris with the Army of the Loire. I am of those who believe it is far wiser for the Army of the Loire and the Army of the North to converge at Rouen, and together move on Paris along the valley of the Seine. But one thing is certain: we must act. Any movement of our provincial armies will force Moltke to detach troops from his over-stretched siege lines. He will be weakened, confused. We must strike at once. We must crush the invader. We must redeem the disaster of Sedan. The shame of the Empire will vanish in the glory of the Republic.

———

I look down at wooded countryside. Here and there a clearing in the trees, a hut with smoke rising in a straight line from a chimney. The top of the smoke shakes a little, looks like unravelling rope. A hawk flies above the trees. We do not know these forests. The compass needle spins like a drunkard. Are there Frenchmen in the woods, waiting to greet us like heroes? Or are there Prussian encampments, gun batteries, soldiers with needle-guns already looking up, taking aim? Vallard believes it is unsafe to land. Prussian cavalry patrols are everywhere. We drift higher, above the unknown forest.

———

Yesterday I walked beyond the ramparts into the Bois de Boulogne. The felling of the great trees for fuel, for barricades, has left new, disturbing vistas: you can see in the distance the white church of Saint-Cloud, bluish smoke rising from smouldering houses. Fields of underbrush, spotted with tree stumps, stretch away. Here and there you see grey canvas tents and huts of fir branches, shirts drying on rope lines. Along the road there is a continual loud rumble of big-wheeled bronze guns drawn by four horses; ammunition wagons; the lighter roll of private carriages carrying sightseers. And in your ears, in your skin, in the soles of your feet, always the roar of cannon from the fort on Mont Valérien.

———

An undulating plain, yellow hopfields and oatfields, brown ploughed farmland, the dark line of a canal. Haystacks with shadows. Clumps of trees. I see a windmill with turning sails, a turning shadow beside it. In the distance, hills purplish and brown. Although I keep a sharp eye out for movement in the trees, it is peaceful here, in the blue air, drifting along. And a wayward desire steals over me: to stay aloft, to live a life in the air, to hover forever between earth and sky. The desire disturbs me. In its heart I detect a secret weakness: this sudden, unaccountable desire, is it not the sign of a weakened will, of the inner wound unhealed? To remain above, to look down, to drift along, to give way, to dream . . . is this not to take sides with indifference, to encourage the rift within? And therefore – sheer logic forces me to such a conclusion – is it not secretly to aid the Prussian cause? The sky is treacherous. I must be vigilant.

———

I fix my gaze below on fields already changing to woods and force myself to think of war. The question of artillery troubles my sleep. Reports from soldiers who fought at Spicheren, Froeschwiller, Saint-Privat, Sedan are deeply disturbing, though perhaps exaggerated. In the confusion of battle, can the truth be known? And yet it appears that the breech-loading Krupp guns, made of steel, have much greater range than our muzzle-loading bronze cannon. Is it possible? The Krupp shells, fitted with percussion caps, explode only on impact, whereas our time-fuse shells explode mostly in the air. It is said that if Moltke gave the order, the Prussian gunners could lob shells into the streets of Paris from the heights of Châtillon, which we lost in September. Why, why, why do we sit and wait? How long will our provisions hold out? Do we wish to trade Paris for a crust of bread? We must attack. Paris is ready and eager. Our soldiers are armed with magnificent breech-loading *chassepot* rifles that are sighted at sixteen hundred yards. Think of it! The soldiers of the first Napoleon, the conquerors of Jena, were equipped with smooth-bore muzzle-loading muskets with a range of scarcely fifty yards! Our rifles are far superior even to the Prussian needle-gun, which brought Austria to its knees. Why do we sit and do nothing? In the woods I see a sudden movement, which appears to be that of an animal, perhaps a deer.

———

Difficult to cast off this feeling of listlessness. Blue air, the shadow of our balloon rippling over trees. And again the desire, not a desire, but the inclination, not an inclination, but rather a picturing, an idle imagining, offspring of silence and blue air. Have I been so deeply wounded? I must not give way. And yet, to live aloft, a floating man, a citizen of the air ... surely it could be done. Touching down from time to time, in a potato field or plum orchard, the basket of the balloon hovering above its anchor; then climbing a rope ladder into my airy home and off into the impalpable element. Easy enough to construct a more civilized basket, with space to sleep, a roof to keep out rain and snow; books; stores of food; writing materials; a rifle; a telescope; a parrot in a cage for companion – a floating island; mobile nest; travelling the world above shifting scenes; the white-capped seas and monkey-chattering jungles; the glittering ice mountains of the north; my bed afloat in blue lakes of sky; never come back; childhood's dream.

I could push Vallard over the side. A quick motion would suffice. He would fall swiftly, turning over and over. An unfortunate accident. The suddenly lightened balloon shoots up, but I pull on the valve rope, calmly. Alone, drifting through the sky. Away from it all. It could be done.

To have had such a thought ... Am I no longer myself? Unmanned by air? Heaven-unhinged! And now – sudden revulsion – the basket fills me with loathing; the rope; the anchor; my hand like a cold claw gripping the rim; I can't bear this place; this voyage; this up-here hovering; the inhuman sky; down, look down; and I feel a prickling in my skin, and I think: to jump, to feel the wind in my hair, to plunge in a rush of wind, to feel myself break against a tree; sweet pain; the bayonet in my throat; blood-gush; earth-smash; anything but this.

All at once we have entered a region of thick, swirling mist. Vallard, half a step from me, has become a ghostly form. Above me the balloon has vanished. The suspension ropes rise into smoke, are erased like lines of chalk. The clouds thicken; my hand disappears. I am invisible to myself. There is nothing in the world but cold damp desolate empty grey and the bite of the basket's rim in my clenched palm. We have died, Vallard and I, we have entered the shadowless realm, region of erasures and absences, kingdom of dissolution. Clumps of cloud-mist enter my mouth like smoke. Here on the other shore, here at the world's end, give me the sight and touch of things: shape of a hand, curve of a chin, weight of a stone; the heft of earthly things. Edges! Edges!

———

At last; out there; a shape in the cloud-soup; and as we drift closer, there below, swathed in the mist-swirl, yes! the top of – a pine?

———

We burst through the clouds, which seem to rush above us in streamers of vapour, and see below a valley, broad and deep, sun-slashed – dazzle of green, splash of yellow and scarlet – patches of mist like smoke. Swords of sun strike from the clouds. We have drifted over a steep hill, bristly with pine. A flock of birds below us, black-blue, flying over their lagging shadows. I look at Vallard, who meets my gaze. An understanding passes between us. Has he felt it too? It's time. He pulls the valve rope, we begin the descent. Shadows like dark lakes lie on the autumn woods and fields. A stream or river, coppery brown, flashes fish scales of sun. On the far hill a tiny farmhouse with a slate roof. Friend or foe? We have been aloft for four hours and thirty-five minutes. It is time. Our compass is crazed, useless, but the wind has shifted so often that no compass could have helped. Are we safely beyond the German lines? Have we reached the north? The west? What is this place? Have we blown as far as Brittany? Is it possible we've drifted east, crossed the border into Belgium? We don't know. So be it! As we descend, I scan the woods for tents, horses, a stray patrol. I see only the play of cloud-shadow on field and wood, the farmhouse silent, a field of stubble, pinewoods. The fat shadow of our balloon glides below, dragging after it the disturbingly small shadow of our basket. Now open meadows appear, tan and yellow among the trees. Mauve shadows. Copses, fields, an outcrop of grey rock. The land rises to meet us as we come slanting down, grows larger, breaks into detail. I begin to make out high straw-coloured grass, wild-flowers purple and white in a sloping field. I look up at the sky, at blue air and drifting cloud, up there where the wide spaces cleave the spirit like an axeblade, I bid the whispering and too-high heavens farewell, then I cast my eyes downwards, towards the rising earth, towards the solid place, the human turmoil.

Paradise park

Paradise Park, which was destroyed by fire on 31 May 1924, except for a number of steel and concrete structures that rose eerily from the blackened ruins until they were torn down the following year, first opened its gates on 1 June 1912, on eight and two-thirds acres of the former site of Dreamland, across Surf Avenue from Luna Park. In an era noted for the brilliance and extravagance of its amusement parks, the new park seemed to be presenting itself as a culmination. Even the diminished acreage, with its mere 652 feet of ocean frontage, proved responsible for many of the park's most striking features, for it was immediately clear that Paradise Park was striving to overcome the limitations of space by a certain flamboyance or excess that pushed it in directions never before undertaken in the architecture of amusement parks.

The first sign that the new owner was prepared to respond boldly to the challenge of his rivals was the four-hundred-foot-high white wall that rose about the newly acquired property, dwarfing Luna's main tower, casting its late-afternoon shadow all the way to Steeplechase and surpassing even the legendary tower of Dreamland, which was said to have been illuminated by one hundred thousand electric lights. In that early era of enclosed amusement parks, Paradise Park was the most visibly and radically enclosed of all. The soaring white wall, composed of staff over a lath-and-iron frame, suggested on the one hand a defiant act of exclusion, an outrageous assertion of privacy, and on the other an invitation, a deliberate titillation or provocation – the latter most clearly in evidence at the towering top of the unadorned wall, which only there, high in the sky, broke into a profusion of colourful towers, minarets, domes and spires.

Two openings pierced the mystery of the great wall: an ocean entrance, across an iron pier and through the grimacing mouth of an immense clown's face, and the Surf Avenue entrance, through a soaring arch flanked by sixty-foot dragons. The openings did not reveal the inside of the park but ushered visitors into a broad, meandering tunnel that wound its way parallel to the wall for hundreds of feet before turning abruptly inward to the park itself. Lit with red, blue and yellow electric lights, the winding tunnel was lined on both sides with ball-and-milk-bottle booths, carnival wheels, Moxie stands, curtained freak shows, gypsy palmist tents, hot roasted corn stalls, phrenology shops displaying maps of skulls divided into zones, tattoo parlours, penny arcades, shooting galleries – all of it ringing with the mingled din of tumbling bottles, rattling balls, Graphophone music, the shouts of barkers ('And a jaunt for joy it is, ladies and gentlemen!') and the muffled clatter of unseen rides. Scattered among the familiar pleasures of Paradise Alley, as the entrance tunnel came to be called, were a number of new and exciting ones that proved highly popular, such as the Sky Cars, small electric-traction elevators lined with black velvet and operated by masked female attendants in scarlet livery who took customers up to the top of the wall for a sudden, magnificent view of the park.

Since secrecy was part of the allure of Paradise Park, the elusive creator-manager, who from the beginning surrounded himself with a certain mystery, permitted no publicity photos in the course of an otherwise vigorous promotional campaign. The historian must therefore rely on a scattering of amateur photographs that focus on particular attractions but give no reliable view of the whole. Despite the absence of a definitive map or plan, it is nevertheless possible to reconstruct the early form of the park in some detail from the many reports, sometimes conflicting, of early witnesses.

What struck the first visitors, as they emerged from Paradise Alley into the park itself, was the powerful upward or vertical thrust. In the bewildering assault of first impressions it was immediately apparent that the park consisted of several levels, to which access was had by numerous stairways, escalators and electric elevators. Each of the two upper levels was a system of wide iron bridges that intersected at one or more points to form broad plazas, large enough to house booths, cafés, brass bands and mechanical rides, as well as a variety of exotic attractions: a Zulu village, a Chinese temple, a Javanese puppet theatre, a replica of the market-place of Marrakesh and a reconstructed village of Mbuti pygmies from the Ituri Forest, including forty-five Mbuti tribesmen living in reassembled native huts. The bridges were supported by a system of openwork iron towers, many of which were supplied with stairways and elevators; the entire structure of bridges and supports left a feeling of openness, so that at any point on the ground one could see big slices of blue sky. Fifty-five elevator shafts in the inner walls gave access to every bridge at both levels, and all around the inner wall rose the spiral of an immense railed stairway, which quickly became known as Paradise Road and led to the top of the wall. There people could walk four abreast along a balustrade lined with game booths and food stands and look down at Paradise Park itself, with its criss-crossing bridges, its festive plazas, its roller-coaster and Ferris wheel, its exotic villages, its enticing spectacles with casts of thousands, such as the Destruction of Carthage and the Burning Skyscraper; or they could gaze outwards at the great beach stretching east and west with its domed and towering hotels, its double-decked iron piers, its bathing pavilions – out beyond the lighthouse at Sea Gate in one direction and the sailboats on Sheepshead Bay in the other, and farther still, much farther, for it was said that on a clear day you could see sixty miles in any direction.

Although from the beginning there were critics of the new park, who argued that the vertical emphasis was reminiscent of the world of skyscrapers and elevated railroads from which the urban visitor longed to escape, the response of the public was decisively enthusiastic. Those who frequented the park began to say they could no longer enjoy single-level parks, which seemed too close to the ground; and so successful was the park that a single ride called the Sidewinder, which cost $86,000 to build, drew $375,000 in receipts in the first three seasons.

If the most striking and immediate fact about Paradise Park was its multilevel verticality, its continual invitation to half-glimpsed excitements high overhead, the crowds soon noticed that the park offered, along with familiar amusements, a number of new attractions. One sensation of the opening season was a brand-new mechanical ride called the Nightmare Railway, a development of the scenic railway and Old Mill in the direction of the House of Horrors. Delighted visitors discovered that the great white wall contained an elaborate set of tracks that rose and fell sharply along a dark, twisting tunnel which presented a series of frights: the car, which held twelve people on six benches, went rushing towards immense boulders that collapsed upon contact, approached another car that suddenly swooped overhead on a second set of tracks, experienced a landslide, a flood, an avalanche and a raging fire, passed through a dragon's den, a mummy's crypt, a haunted grave-yard, a cave of malignant dwarfs and a vampire's castle, and emerged at last in a bright opening two hundred feet above the ground of Paradise Park.

Even more popular than the new mechanical rides was an entirely new group of amusements called Adventures. An Adventure, according to the promotional material, was not a ride but a carefully re created real-life experience: for ten cents one could enter the Dark Forest and be attacked by a gang of bandits, or step into the Streets of Lisbon and experience the famous earthquake, or wander through Old Algeria and experience the thrill of being surrounded by angry Moslems, tied up in a burlap sack, carried off on the back of a camel and dangled over a cliff above crashing waves. One of the more popular Adventures was Lovers' Leap, a three-hundred-foot-high rocky cliff (staff over lath and iron) that rose at one corner of the park and offered to daredevil couples a fearful ledge jutting out over a thundering waterfall that threw up great clouds of spray; the sound of the roaring water was produced by machines concealed in the artificial cliff and the thick spray was sent up through dozens of holes in the staff. The couples who jumped shrieking into the thundering mist were caught ten feet below in a concealed net that broke their fall lightly and carried them eighty feet down into the swirling mist, where muscular attendants released them and guided them into a descending elevator.

But the single most popular attraction of the 1912 season proved rather surprisingly to be an immense model of the resort itself, done in precise scale and measuring thirty by twenty-five feet. Located on a plaza of the third level and surrounded by roped pedestrian walks supplied with coin-operated telescopes, the model showed Coney Island in May of 1911, just before the fire that destroyed Dreamland. In brilliant detail it replicated the heart of Coney Island from Steeplechase Park to Dreamland, including Surf Avenue, Mermaid Avenue, the host of side-streets with their saloons and music halls, their dance pavilions and hotels, their shooting galleries and souvenir shops, and the beach itself with its double-decked iron piers and its bath-houses, all populated by tiny automatons (the brass band played, the man in the straw boater shot the tin duck in the row of moving ducks, the girl on the roller-coaster opened her mouth and rolled her eyes). The detail was so scrupulous that the model was said to duplicate every tie in every track of every roller-coaster, every waxwork in the Eden Musée, including the pastework pearls of Jenny Lind, and every slat in every rocking chair on the porch of every hotel; and it was rumoured that with the aid of a penny-in-the-slot telescope you could see not only the precise replication of every ornate machine in every penny arcade and the minuscule letters of every peepshow entertainment (*Actors and Models, After the Bath, Bare in the Bear Skin, What the Book Agent Saw*) but, through the elegantly duplicated peepshow viewer, the flickering, teasingly vague black-and-white pictures themselves. The highly popular model was the work of Otis Stilwell, a carver of carousel horses who as a hobby made lovingly detailed miniature merry-go-rounds, roller-coasters and fun-houses that he sold in a shop on Surf Avenue and who, along with the inventor Otto Danziker, was to prove one of the owner-manager's closest advisers. The minia-ture Coney Island, which attracted amazed attention as a kind of wondrous toy, served a deeper purpose: by reducing the entire resort to a miniature within his amusement park, the manager was enhancing the size and power of his park, which became a gigantic and marvellous structure stretching away in every direction; at the same time he was inviting the admiring crowds to experience a subtle condescension towards all rival attractions, which were reduced to charming toys.

Like other amusement-park entrepreneurs at the turn of the century, the owner-manager of Paradise Park was confronted by the problem of attracting a mass audience hungry for pleasure and excitement while excluding any threat to the supposed values of that audience, such as the prostitutes, gamblers and gangsters who flourished on every Coney Island side-street. By enclosing their parks and hiring enforcement squads, the entrepreneurs were able to exercise unprecedented control, but the astute manager noted a new problem: the new, safe pleasures of the enclosed parks threatened to make them too tame and predictable, to push them in the unfortunate direction of the genteel beer garden. This problem he solved brilliantly by hiring a troupe of eighteen hundred specially trained actors to imitate the rowdiness and vice whose exclusion had left a secret yearning. Hence the park included among its attractions a number of dark saloons, seedy roadhouses and crooked alleys lined by dubious shops, in which customers could mingle with prostitutes, pickpockets, cutthroats, drunken sailors, pimps, con men and gangland thugs, assured that the racy language, the shocking costumes and the terrifying fights which periodically erupted were part of the show. Actresses playing the part of prostitutes were particularly admired by male and female visitors, who enjoyed seeing at close range the disturbing, thrilling streetwalkers with their invitation to forbidden pleasures that were strictly and safely imaginary. Patrons who themselves became rowdy or offensive were swiftly removed by the very efficient park police, who roamed the grounds in uniform or in disguise. Because the distinction was not always clear between an actor dressed like a sailor with a false tattoo on his forearm and a real sailor with a real tattoo, or an actress with rouged cheeks and brazen eyes strutting along the booth-lined alleys and a factory girl from Brooklyn wearing a new chinchilla coat and a straw hat with a willow plume, a certain heady confusion was experienced by the park's patrons, who began to feel that they too were actors and actresses disguised as seamstresses, schoolteachers, department-store clerks, typists and shopkeepers – roles that they no longer took as seriously as they did in that other world of work and tiredness.

Among the many disguises in Paradise Park were those of the owner-manager himself, for it quickly became known that the secretive proprietor liked to mingle unseen with the crowds in order to observe the operation of his park at close range, overhear responses to his amusements, and imagine rearrangements and improvements. Disguised as a park workman in cap, shirt-sleeves and vest, an Irish shopkeeper in his Sunday bowler, a uniformed trombone player in epaulettes, a city swell in striped pants, bow tie and straw boater, a bearded Jew in a long coat of black gabardine, the manager would make the rounds of his park, studying the crowd and devising ways to improve congested areas. Once, overhearing a couple complain that the Lovers' Leap was disappointing because the concealed net broke the fall too soon, he had the net lowered by ten feet and discovered that revenues increased. As rumours of his presence persisted, visitors began to search for the disguised owner-manager among the throngs; and people began to wonder a little about the man who walked among them unseen, listening to them, observing them and seeking to increase their delight.

They knew only that he was an outsider, from Manhattan, who had come late to the amusement-park business and who, it was said, had money to burn. Then a journalist named Warren Burchard wrote a long article that appeared in a special Coney Island supplement of the *Brooklyn Eagle* (10 August 1912). In the course of analysing Coney Island amusements, calculating trends, reporting revenues and discussing patterns of crowd behaviour, Burchard devoted several paragraphs to the latest proprietor of 'marvellous Coney', Charles Sarabee. Sarabee, Burchard reported, was a native New Yorker who was yet another instance of that peculiarly American phenomenon, the self-made man. Sarabee's father had sold cigars in the shop of a small Manhattan hotel. As a boy Charles had worked long hours in the cigar shop, where by the age of nine he had not only mastered the bewildering array of names, prices and cedar-wood box covers, but had begun to arrange cigars in eye-catching displays, the most successful of which was a three-foot-high wire tree hung with Christmas ornaments and high-priced Havanas. At thirteen he went to work as a bellhop at the hotel. There his efficiency, industry and cleverness endeared him to the manager and earned him a series of promotions starting with desk clerk and ending, when Charles was twenty-one, with the post of assistant manager, in which capacity he introduced a wide variety of improvements, including fruit trees in every lobby and, in every bathroom, up-to-date fixtures in stylish settings: mahogany-hooded shower-baths, heated brass towel-rails and Ionic pilasters of Siena marble. His big break came several years later when as manager-owner of the hotel he decided to enter a partnership in a new downtown department store. He soon had the controlling interest in three other department stores, but his fortune was made at the age of thirty, when he introduced in his stores a revolutionary idea called the 'leisure spot'. Sarabee had always had a sharp eye for the behaviour of customers, and he had noticed that many of them grew tired and irritable after an hour or two of strolling from department to department and riding elevators and escalators in search of something they thought they wanted but probably didn't need. He knew it was important to keep his customers cheerful and in a free-spending mood, but even more important than this was simply to keep them in the store for as long as possible. Thus arose the idea of leisure spots: small oases of comfort located on every floor, where customers could relax in pleasant surroundings and recover from the tremendous assault on the nervous system represented by the modern department store with its countless treasures temptingly displayed. The leisure spots would attempt to simulate the atmosphere of a cosy living-room, with thick armchairs and couches, crocheted pillows, lace antimacassars, mahogany lamp tables on which stood porcelain lamps with tasseled shades, and in one corner a smiling, apple-cheeked young woman in a crisp blue uniform who sold steaming cups of tea and coffee and a variety of tarts, cakes, cookies and gingerbread. Although the leisure spots took up valuable floor space and proved forbiddingly expensive to install, they turned out to be immensely popular, and after a month it was clear that customers were staying longer and spending more. Rival stores quickly imitated the new device, but Sarabee's leisure spots were always more appealing and he took care to vary them in order to overcome monotony: in quick succession he introduced leisure spots in the style of an English pub, a Dutch cottage, a Victorian parlour, a Japanese tearoom and an Alpine chalet. Inspired by his successes, he soon began to introduce more fanciful décors, such as the Amazon jungle, the Italian plaza, the Puritan village and the hold of a whaling ship, all designed with extreme fidelity, if not to History herself, then to the public's romantic idea of each exotic place. His search for new ideas led him to visit world's fairs and expositions, where the reproduction of exotic places had become fashionable, as well as the big Eastern pleasure resorts that borrowed themes and purchased properties from defunct expositions; and in 1908, on a trip to Coney Island, which he had not visited since his childhood, and where he attempted without success to purchase the old three-hundred-foot-high Iron Tower that had once been the showpiece of the Philadelphia Centennial Exposition of 1876, he was struck by the festive architecture of the three new amusement parks – Steeplechase, Luna and Dreamland – as well as by the immense, lively and free-spending crowds. He had been growing a little stale in the department-store business; he needed a new outlet for his energies. The destruction of Dreamland Park by fire in the spring of 1911 was decisive. As the city hesitated to purchase the ruined grounds put up for sale by the Dreamland Corporation, who proposed that the fifteen acres of Dreamland and the fifteen additional acres destroyed by fire should be turned into a public park, Sarabee was able to arrange for the lease of eight and two-thirds acres of the former amusement park, with the stipulation that the lease would be terminated when public development began, an event that was delayed until the administration of Fiorello La Guardia in 1934, while the remaining acres, during the intervening years, were operated as a parking lot.

With the instinct of a true showman, Sarabee understood that the fatal enemy of amusement is boredom, and he was tireless in his search for new mechanical rides, new spectacles, new thrills and excitements. Working closely with the inventor Otto Danziker, who had designed the Nightmare Railway, Sarabee introduced at least five major rides each season, dismantling any that failed to prove successful. Of the thirteen new rides presented at Paradise Park in the second two seasons (1913 and 1914) before the breakthrough of 1915, one of the most popular was the Swizzler, a three-hundred-foot-high openwork iron column containing a spiral track down which cars holding ten people rushed at terrifying speeds, only to crash through a floor straight into a twisting black tunnel that suddenly burst into light around a bend and revealed that the car was about to rush into a brick wall. At the last second a door in the wall sprang open to reveal a track plunging into a lake, which proved to be an optical illusion projected by tilted mirrors reflecting a movie of rippling lakewater; at the bottom of the track the car slowed and entered a small room that rose into the air – the room was a hydraulic elevator – and released the car into a tunnel that led through suddenly opened doors into a sunny opening at the base of the column. Other successful rides created by Danziker were the Tumbler, the Spider, the Whim-Wham, the Flip, the Lightnin' Lizzie and the Crazy Wheel – this last a gigantic horizontal ring of steel over one hundred feet in diameter, balanced on a pivot so that it turned like a great, wobbling coin, and supplied with hanging, swinging seats on the inner and outer rims. Danziker also designed a special Ferris wheel that slowly rotated like a top while turning vertically, and he placed a medium-sized roller-coaster on a plaza of the second level, some three hundred feet in the air, which Sarabee promptly advertised as the world's highest roller-coaster.

By the end of the third season the box-office take made it clear that Paradise Park had achieved an unprecedented success and had begun to attract a significant portion of the Steeple-chase and Luna crowds. The exciting new rides, the lure of the upper levels, the eighteen hundred actors, the sense of being in a place that was unlike any other place on earth but also reassuringly familiar, all this promised a triumphant future, and the outbreak of the European war, which some had feared might harm the amusement business, proved only a further impetus to pleasure. People speculated on the rides already said to be under construction for next season and a journalist reported, on dubious evidence, that Sarabee was going to unveil an entirely new kind of ride. The rumour was in fact mistaken, for Sarabee and Danziker were planning a number of sophisti-cated mechanical rides that broke no new technological ground; but in a broad sense the rumour proved to be true, for it was during the last week of the 1914 season that a small incident occurred which led to a startling new development in Paradise Park.

A workman called Ed O'Hearn, who had been sent into the tunnel beneath the Swizzler on a routine check of the track, pulled a handkerchief out of his pocket to wipe some dirt from his face. He dislodged a dime, which began rolling down a packed-earth incline beside the track. O'Hearn had been plan-ning to spend his dime on a hot dog with mustard and sauerkraut, and he hurried after it with his electric lantern. He saw the dime come to a stop some fifteen feet below him, but when he reached the spot, the dime had disappeared. O'Hearn crawled about on his knees and patted the hard earth with his palm. As he did so he was surprised to feel a current of cool air streaming upwards. He lowered the lantern and saw a fissure in the earth about two feet long and the width of a finger. When he dropped a flat stone sideways into the crack he counted to twenty before he heard a faint sound. He immediately returned above-ground to report to his boss, who sent a message to Sarabee.

An hour later a team of three engineers investigated the crevice and determined that a small limestone cavity existed far beneath the Swizzler but posed no danger to the ride or to the park itself. Sarabee, disguised as one of the engineers, withdrew into a kind of sombre brooding. When one of his men tried to reassure him that the park was perfectly safe, Sarabee is reported to have said: 'It's all clear now. What'd you say?'

Thus was born the idea that was to give to the history of the amusement park a certain swerve that some found dubious but that no one was able to ignore. All fall and winter the great plans were laid; in his park office on Surf Avenue, Sarabee met daily with Otto Danziker, Otis Stilwell and the engineer William Engelstein. The project was carried forward with characteristic secrecy, and indeed it remains one of the remarkable facts about Sarabee that he was able to elicit from everyone who worked for him an unfailing loyalty. Two weeks before the start of the new season, red-and-black posters appeared in the windows of restaurants and dance halls, on hoardings and telephone poles, on hotel notice-boards and the walls of bathhouses, announcing a NEW PARADISE PARK: *You Have to See It to Believe It*. On opening day the great entrance remained closed; a barker with cane and striped derby announced from a platform sixty feet high that the park would open one week later, on 29 May. Rumour had it that the delay was a promotional gimmick aimed at increasing the air of mystery that surrounded the park; there was talk of a new kind of roller-coaster, a more thrilling fun-house; and some said that Sarabee himself, with cane and striped derby, had announced the delay from the platform between the heads of the great dragons that flanked the closed entrance.

The gates opened on 29 May 1915, at eight in the morning; by noon the crowd had exceeded one hundred thousand. People who had visited the park before were puzzled and disappointed. Apart from three new rides, including a splendid Haunted Mountain, and a new sideshow consisting entirely of midgets (a midget Fat Lady, a midget Ossified Man, a midget Wild Man of Borneo, a midget Bearded Lady, a pair of midget Siamese twins), nothing about the park seemed new enough to merit the publicity campaign. Visitors did, however, notice a number of odd-looking structures scattered about. Each structure was a rotunda composed of columns with grotesque capitals – grimacing devils, weeping clown faces, winged lions and horses, struggling mermaids fondled by hairy monkeys, three-headed chickens – roofed with a gilt dome, on top of which sat a miniature Danziker merry-go-round turning to barrel-organ melodies. Each of the dozen rotundas contained a central pole, a circle of wooden benches and a uniformed attendant. When people were seated on the benches, which held as many as forty, the attendant pulled a lever in the pole, causing the platform to descend rapidly through a cylindrical shaft. At the bottom of the shaft the benches suddenly flattened out, the floor began to turn and whirling, laughing, frightened people began spinning off the edge down any of fourteen chutes that led to a red curtain – and as they passed through the curtain they saw, all around them, as an attendant helped them to their feet at the bottom of the slide, a vast underground amusement park.

This immense subterranean project, with its roller-coaster and fun-house, its tents and pavilions, its spires and domes and minarets, all lit by electric lights and alive with carousel music,

the shouts of barkers, the rattle of rides and even the smell of
the sea, had been designed by Engelstein with the help of
engineers who had worked on the Boston and New York City
subway systems, and had been carried out by a force of nearly
two thousand Irish, Italian and Polish immigrant labourers
lowered into shafts with pickaxes, shovels and wheelbarrows, as
well as by teams of trained workers who laid charges of
dynamite to blast through boulders or operated a hydraulic
tunnel-shield designed by Danziker for boring through clay and
quicksand. In the course of excavation workmen discovered the
jaw of a mastodon, a casket of seventeenth-century Dutch coins
and the rusty anchor of a Dutch merchant ship. The final
structure appears to have been a skilful mixture of broad tunnels
serving as fairground midways and high, open stretches roofed
in reinforced concrete lined with dark blue tiles to resemble a
night sky in summer. The completed park included at one end a
great beach of white sand and an artificial ocean – in reality a
great shallow basin filled with ocean water and containing
Danziker's wave machine, which caused long, perfectly breaking waves to fall on the flawless beach. Two immense hotels, a
band pavilion and half a dozen bathhouses lined the beach, and
a great iron pier with shops and restaurants under its wooden
roof stretched twelve hundred feet into the water. Five hundred
seagulls brought down from the upper shore added a realistic
touch, though later it was discovered that the birds did not
prosper in the subterranean world and gave birth to sickly
offspring with wobbly walks and crazed flight patterns, who
frightened children and had to be replaced by fresh gulls and
hand-painted balsawood models. High above the beach, and
the piers, and the park, and the always burning electric lights
stretched the night sky of blue-black tiles, supplied with
thousands of twinkling artificial stars and a brilliant moon
emerging from and disappearing behind slow-moving clouds
beamed up by hidden projectors.

The creation of an underground amusement park with an ocean setting may have been a triumph of engineering, but Sarabee was too shrewd to rely solely on first impressions. His underground park had features that distinguished it clearly from his upper park, so that customers, after the first shock of delight or admiration, did not grow impatient, did not feel cheated. In addition to four new rides, including the wildly popular Yo-Yo, an immense steel yo-yo suspended by a thick cable from a tower and supplied with seats, visitors to Sarabee's Bargain Basement, as the new park good-naturedly came to be called, discovered that many rides and attractions were playful or fiendish variations of familiar amusement-park pleasures. Thus the merry-go-round included an all-white horse that turned out to be a bucking bronco, around a high curve the roller-coaster left the tracks and soared over a twenty-foot gap to another set of tracks (such at least was the thrilling sensation, although in fact the cars were supported from beneath by hinged beams attached to the coaster frame), the fun-house mirrors turned people into hideous, frightening monsters and the Ferris wheel, at the climax of the ride, dropped slowly from its stationary supports and rolled back and forth along a track that left room for the bottom-most cars to pass unharmed. In the same spirit the architecture was more extravagant – the front roller-coaster cars were supplied with carved dragon's heads, the Old Mill began in the sneering mouth of an ogre, a papier-mâché mountain called the Haunted Grotto opened at a cave flanked by thirty-foot naked giantesses whose legs and arms were encircled by giant snakes – and the stage properties for the actors were more sinister, the actor-drunks rowdier, the false prostitutes more brazen, some going so far as to lure customers into back rooms that turned out to be part of the House of Mirth. The sense that the rides were, in a controlled way, out of control, that they were exceeding bounds, that they were imitating nightmarish breakdowns while remaining perfectly safe, all this proved intoxicating to the crowds, who at the same time were urged to a feverish carnival spirit by the winking electric lights, the artificial night sky, the crash of artificial waves, the sense of a vast underground adventure not bound by the rules of ordinary parks.

Despite the enthusiastic reception of Sarabee's New Paradise Park by Coney Island pleasure-seekers, by journalists and by a number of distinguished foreign visitors, several critical voices were raised during the first months, and not only from the ranks of observers who might be expected to cast doubt on the new institutions of mass pleasure such as the dance hall, the vaudeville theatre, the movie house and the amusement park. An article in the August 1915 issue of *Munsey's Magazine* praised New Paradise Park for the boldness of its design and the ingenuity of its rides but paused to question whether Sarabee had not pushed the amusement park beyond its proper limit. Such developments as the leaping roller-coaster and the rolling Ferris wheel, though of undoubted technological interest, threatened to make people bored with traditional rides and to encourage in them an unhealthy appetite for more extreme and dangerous sensations. It was in this sense that technology and morality became related issues, for a mass audience accustomed to violent mechanical pleasures was in danger of growing dissatisfied with the routines of everyday life and especially with their jobs, a dissatisfaction that in turn was bound to lead to a desire for more extreme forms of release. For finally the carefully engineered mechanical excitements and sensual stimulations of Sarabee's park were not and could not be satisfying, but were in the nature of a cheat, an ingenious illusion that left people secretly restless and unappeased. The unsigned article concluded by wondering whether this abiding restlessness was not the true aim of the great amusement-park showman, in whose interest it was to create an audience perpetually hungry for the unfruitful pleasures he knew so well how to provide.

Even as such questions were being raised by voices sceptical of the new mass culture in general and of New Paradise Park in particular, it was rumoured that Sarabee and his staff were at work on new plans, and there were those who said that Sarabee would never rest until he had carried the amusement park to its farthest limit of expression.

The new stage in the evolution of Paradise Park was not completed for two years, during which attendance increased even as war threatened. Unlike the upper park, the underground park was not required to close after the summer season and Sarabee was able to run it at a profit through mid-November, after which the thinning crowds forced him to close for the winter. In the profitable season of 1916 three new rides appeared in the underground park, including a Ferris wheel supplied with paired carousel horses instead of seats, while in the upper park small signs of a disturbing development first became noticeable. The rides, although still in operation, were no longer replaced by new ones; the high roller-coaster suffered a mechanical breakdown and was shut down; here and there a booth stood empty. Although the lawns and paths around the famous rotundas were kept clean and neat, grass grew wild in far corners of the park and occasional patches of rust appeared on brightly painted steel frames.

It was in the expanded park of 1917 that Sarabee achieved what many called the fulfilment of his dream, although a few voices were raised in dissent. Visitors to the famous underground park discovered, in scattered and unlikely locations – on the beach, in bathhouses, behind game booths, under the roller-coaster – some two dozen escalators leading down. The simple escalators led to a second underground level where a puzzling new park had been created – a pastoral park of oak and beech woodlands, winding paths, peaceful lakes, rolling hills,

flowering meadows, babbling brooks, wooden footbridges and
soothing waterfalls: a detailed artificial landscape composed
entirely of plaster and pasteboard (except for an occasional
actor-shepherd with his herd of real sheep), illuminated by the
light of electric lanterns with coloured glass panes, and inviting
the tired reveller to solitude and meditation. This deliberate
emphasis on pleasures opposed to those of the amusement park
was not lost upon visitors, who savoured the contrast but could
not overcome a sense of disappointment. That carefully arranged dissatisfaction was in turn overcome when the visitor
on his ramble discovered an opening in a hill, or a doorway in
an old oak, or a tunnel in a riverbank, all of which contained
stone steps that led down to another level, where at the end of
rocky passageways with mossy mouths a brilliant new amusement park stretched away.

Here in a masterful mingling of attractions visitors were
invited to ride the world's first spherical Ferris wheel; experience
the thrilling sensation of being buried alive in a coffin in the
Old Graveyard; visit a Turkish palace, including the secret
rooms of the seraglio with over six hundred concubines; ride
the exciting new Wild Wheel Coaster; visit an exact reproduction of the Alhambra with all its pillars, arches, courtyards and
gardens, including the seventy-five-foot-high dome of the Salo
de los Embajadores and the Patio de los Leones with its alabaster
fountain supported by twelve white marble lions; enter the
world's most frightening House of Horrors with its unforgettable Hall of Rats; witness the demonic possession of the girls at
the witch trials of Salem; fly through the trees on the backs of
mechanical monster-birds in the Forest of Night; ride a real
burro down a replicated Grand Canyon trail; visit a bustling
harbour containing reconstructions of a Nantucket whaling
ship, a Spanish galleon, Darwin's *Beagle*, a Viking long ship,
Oliver Hazard Perry's flagship *Lawrence*, a Phoenician trireme, a
Chinese junk and Old Ironsides; see a departed dear one during

a séance in the Medium's Mansion; ride the sensational triple-decker merry-go-round; visit a medieval torture chamber and see actor-victims broken on the rack, crushed in the iron boot and hoisted on the strappado; descend into a replica of the labyrinthine salt mines of Hallstatt, Austria; ride the death-defying Barrel, a padded iron barrel guided by cables along white-water rapids and down a reconstruction of the Horseshoe Falls composed of real Niagara water; ride the Swirl-a-Whirl, the Hootchie-Kootchie and the Coney Island Sling; and pay a heart-warming visit to the Old Plantation, where seventy-five genuine southern darkies (actually white actors in blackface) strummed banjos, danced breakdowns, ate watermelons, picked cotton and sang spirituals in four-part harmony while a benign Master sat on a veranda between his blond-ringletted daughter and a faithful black mammy who from time to time said 'Lawdee!'

This continually changing landscape of rides, spectacles, exotic places and reconstructed cultural wonders was connected by an intricate system of cable cars designed by Danziker, which criss-crossed the entire park and permitted visitors to gain an overview of the multitude of attractions and travel conveniently from one section to another. Danziker had also designed a scale-model subway, consisting of roofless cars the size of scenic-railway cars, driven by real engines and underlying the entire park, with twenty-four stations indicated by small kiosks in twenty-four different styles, including a circus tent, a Gothic cathedral, a tepee, a Persian summerhouse, a log cabin and a Moorish palace.

In addition to the striking transportation system, certain features of the new park drew attention in the popular press, in particular the group of sixteen new mechanical rides invented by Danziker, of which the most successful was the Chute Ball: an openwork iron sphere twenty feet in diameter that rolled along a steep, curving chute while riders inside were seated on twelve benches attached in such a way that they remained upright while revolving on a spindle. It was noted that most of the traditional rides had been carried to further degrees of evolution: in the Double Coaster, specially built roller-coaster cars rounding a turn suddenly rushed from the track and soared unsupported over dangerous gaps onto the track of a second roller-coaster, and an immense and swiftly turning Airplane Swing released its planes one by one to fly through the air to a powerful plane-catching machine that resembled an iron octo-pus. The popular Wild Wheel was seen as a combination of roller-coaster and Ferris wheel: along a sinuous coasterlike track rolled a great iron wheel, forty feet in diameter; the wheel's two grooved rims turned along a pair of steel cables that had been suspended at intervals from wrought-iron posts and ran like telephone wires above the entire length of the dipping and rising track; up to one hundred riders sat strapped into wire cages on the inside of the wheel and turned as the wheel turned. But technological process was less evident in the mechanical rides, which at best were clever variations of familiar rides, than in the methods of transportation, in the advanced plumbing system in the public bathrooms and in minor effects, such as the much-praised pack of mechanical rats in the House of Horrors.

The new park was also praised for its many meticulous reconstructions of cultural landmarks and natural wonders, all of which made the similar attractions of Luna and the exposi-tions seem crude and childish. Sarabee's customers were invited to visit not only the Alhambra, but also the Porcelain Tower of Nanking, the catacombs of Alexandria, the Inca ruins of Cuzco, the hanging gardens of Babylon and the palace of Kubla Khan, as well as an alp, a fjord, a stalactite cavern, a desert containing an oasis, a redwood forest, an iceberg, a sea grotto and a bamboo grove inhabited by real pandas. One of the most admired replicas was that of the Edison Laboratory at West Orange, New Jersey, with its three-storey main building that contained machine shops, experimental rooms, and rooms for glassblowing and electrical testing, as well as the famous forty-foot-high library with its great fireplace and its displays of thousands of ores and minerals in glass-fronted cabinets, the whole building and its four outbuildings enclosed by a high fence with a guard at the entrance gate; the laboratory was supplied with a staff of sixty actor-assistants and Edison himself was played by the Shakespearean actor Howard Ford, who was particularly good at imitating Edison's famous naps – after which he would spring up refreshed and invent the phonograph or the electric light. But Sarabee's mania for replication reached its culmination in an immense project that he designed with Otis Stilwell: a sixty-by-forty-foot model in wood and pasteboard of Paris, France, including over eighty thousand buildings and thirty thousand trees (representing thirty-six different species), the precise furnishings of every apartment, shop, church, café and department store, all the fruits and vegetables in Les Halles and all the fishing nets in the Seine, all the horse-drawn carriages, motor cars, bicycles, fiacres, motor omnibuses and electric streetcars, every tombstone in Père Lachaise cemetery and every plant in the Jardin des Plantes, over two hundred thousand miniature waxwork figures representing all social classes and occupations, and at the heart of the little city, an exact scale model of the Louvre, including not only every gallery, every staircase, every window mullion and ceiling decoration, but a precise miniature reproduction of every painting (oil on copper) and its frame (beechwood), every statue (ivory) and every artefact, from Egyptian sarcophagi to richly detailed eighteenth-century spoons so minuscule that they were invisible to the naked eye and had to be viewed through magnifying lenses.

The 1917 park was widely regarded as the most complete, most successful form of the modern amusement park, its final and classic expression, which might be varied and expanded but never surpassed; and the sole question that remained was where Sarabee would go from here.

Even as the classic park was being hailed in the press, Sarabee was said to be planning another park, about which he was more than usually secretive. At about the same time he began to lose interest in his older parks, which were placed under the management of a five-man board who were required to report to Sarabee only twice a year and who concentrated their attention on the first two underground parks and the pastoral park between them, while largely neglecting the above-ground park, which continued to decline. Patches of rust spread on the bridge-braces, paint peeled on the carousels, weeds grew under the roller-coaster and between lanes of booths; and there were signs of deeper neglect. In certain stretches of the upper park, guards were removed and brought below; the remaining guards grew less vigilant, so that a dangerous element began to assert itself. A gang of actors, who seemed to have grown into their roles, prowled the darkened alleyways, where shanty brothels were said to spring up; and complaints were made against a gang of dwarf thugs who quit the Nightmare Railway and took up residence in a dark corner of the park called Dwarftown, where no one ventured after dusk.

Sarabee's new park, which opened in 1920 beneath the classic park of 1917, puzzled his admirers and caused lengthy reassessments of the showman's career. Here at one blow he did away with the four central features of the modern amusement park – the mechanical ride (roller-coaster, Swizzler), the exotic attraction (replicated village, market, garden, temple), the spectacle (Destruction of Carthage) and the carnival amusement (freak show, game booth) – and replaced them with an entirely new realm of pleasures. In a dramatic turn away from meticulous replication, Sarabee presented to customers in his new underground level a scrupulously fantastic world. And here it becomes difficult to be precise, for Sarabee banned photographs and the historian is forced to rely on often contradictory eyewitness accounts, tainted at times by rumour and exaggeration. We hear of dream-landscapes with gigantic nightmare flowers and imaginary flying animals, of impalpable pillars and edible discs of light. There are reports of sudden stairways leading to underwater kingdoms, of disappearing towns, of vast complex structures that resemble nothing ever seen before. Illusionary effects appear to have been widely used, for we hear of high walls that suddenly melt away, of metamorphoses and vanishings and of a device that made a strong impression: a springing monster suddenly stops in midair, as if frozen, and then dissolves. This last suggests that Sarabee made use of hidden movie projectors to enhance his other effects. The entire park appears to have been a thorough rejection not only of the replica, the reconstruction, the exotic imitation, which had haunted amusement parks from the beginning, but also of the mechanical ride, which by its very nature proclaimed its kinship with the real world of steel, dynamos and electrical power even while turning that world into play. Sarabee's new park seized instead on the unreality and other-worldliness of amusement parks and carried fantastic effects to an unprecedented development. But Sarabee was careful to avoid certain traditional elements of fantasy that had become familiar and cosy. We therefore never hear of comfortable creatures like dragons, witches, ghosts and Martians, or even of familiar elements of fantasy architecture such as pinnacles, towers and battlements. Everything is strange, unsettling, even shifting – for we hear of lighting effects that cause entire structures to be viewed differently, of uncanny replacements and transformations that resemble scene-shifting in a theatre. Machinery appears to have been used solely in a disguised, invisible way; for only the presence of hidden machinery can explain certain repeatedly mentioned phenomena, such as solid islands floating in the air and a mysteriously sinking hill.

The response by the public to Sarabee's new park was curious: people descended, roamed about, uttered admiring sounds, felt a little puzzled and finally returned to one of the higher parks. The opening-day attendance was the highest ever – over sixty-three thousand in the first two hours – but it quickly became apparent that crowds were not staying. By the second month receipts were far below those of even the uppermost park, in its state of increasing neglect. People seemed to admire the new park but not really to like it very much; they preferred the mechanical rides, the replicas, the booths, the barkers, the hot-dog stands, all of which had been rigorously banished from the new park. Sarabee, always alert to the mood of crowds, did what he had never done before: instead of making alterations, he launched a mid-season promotional campaign. Attendance rose for one week, then took a dramatic plunge, and long before the end of the season it was clear that the new park was a resounding failure.

Sarabee met with his staff of advisers, who recommended three kinds of remedy: the addition of exciting new rides to enliven the somewhat inert park; the construction of a huge domed amphitheatre in the centre of the park, to contain twelve tiers of game booths, food stands, shops, restaurants and penny arcades surrounding three revolving stages on which would be presented, respectively, a fun-house, an old-fashioned amusement park and a three-ring circus; and the razing of the park and its replacement by an entirely new one on more conventional lines but with brand-new rides. Sarabee listened attentively, rejected all three recommendations, and shut himself up with Danziker and Stilwell to consider improvements that would enhance rather than alter the nature of the park. In an interview given in 1927, Danziker said that Sarabee had never seemed surer of himself than in this matter of the new park; and despite his own conviction that the park was a failure and that Sarabee should listen to the voice of the people,

Danziker had laid his doubts aside and thrown himself willingly into Sarabee's effort to save the park, which had already begun to be known as Sarabee's Folly.

The enhanced park opened the next season, to a massive publicity campaign that promised people thrills and pleasures of a kind they had never experienced before; a journalist writing in the *New York Herald* called the new park the most brilliant revolution in the history of the amusement park, with effects so extraordinary that they were worthy of the name of art. The next day a journalist on a rival paper asked scornfully: It may be art, but is it fun? He granted the superiority, even the brilliance, of Sarabee's latest devices, but felt that Sarabee had lost touch with the amusement-park spirit, which after all was a popular spirit and thrived on noise, laughter and rough-and-tumble effects. Within a month it was obvious that the refurbished park was not a success. Sarabee continued to run it at a loss, refused to alter it in any way and began to spend several hours a day walking in the shifting dream-perspectives of his nearly empty park, which still drew a small number of visitors, some of whom came solely in the hope of catching a glimpse of the famous entrepreneur. And a rumour began to grow that Sarabee was already making plans for an entirely new park, which would surpass his own most stunning creations and restore him to his rightful place as the Edison of amusement-park impresarios.

In the world of commercial amusement, success is measured in profit; but it is also measured in something less tangible, which may be called approval, or esteem, or fame, but which is really a measure of the world's compliance in permitting a private dream to become a public fact. Sarabee, who had made his fortune in department stores and had since made it many times over in his series of unrivalled parks, had always enjoyed the pleasurable sense that his dreams and inspirations were encouraged by the outer world, were so to speak confirmed and made possible by something outside himself that was greater than himself – namely, the mass of other people who recognized in his embodied dream their own vague dreams, who showered him with money as a sign of their pleasure and for whom he was, in a way, dreaming. His newest park was Sarabee's first experience of commercial failure – his first experience, that is, of losing the world's approval, of dreaming the wrong dream. His peculiar stubbornness may be explained in many ways, but one way is simply this, that he refused to believe what had happened. He kept expecting the crowds to come round. When it became clear they wouldn't, he was already so soaked in his dream that he could not undream it. This is only another way of suggesting that Sarabee, whatever he was, was not cynical; his showmanship, his shrewd sense of what was pleasing to crowds, his painstaking efforts to adjust his inventions in the direction of wider and wider audiences, were only the practical and necessary expression of a cause he thoroughly believed in.

Admirers of Sarabee praised the failed park as a sign of his originality and of his growing independence from the corruptions of mass taste; critics regretted it as a sign of decline, of increasing remoteness from common humanity; but both camps agreed that the failure was a crucial moment in Sarabee's career, a moment that whetted their appetite for his next advance. For there was never any question of that. As Sarabee wandered the shifting illusions of his nearly deserted park, disguised as a weeping clown, or a journalist, or an old man with a cane, who dared to imagine that he hadn't already begun to plan another park?

It was about this time that the board of managers made an effort to save the declining upper park, if only because it served as entrance to the lower levels. Guards in maroon jackets were posted along the paths leading to the rotundas. The high grass was trimmed at the base of the openwork iron towers and under the roller-coaster, bare patches were seeded and paths new-tarred, booths cleaned and painted, rust on bridge-braces removed, roller-coaster tracks repaired and old cars replaced with shiny new ones. Only at the far corners of the park, in the dark, twisting alleys of Dwarftown or the decaying lanes inhabited by unsavoury actors, did the board abandon its efforts at restoring order and permit a shantytown to flourish among the weeds, the refuse, the broken lights.

Eyewitness accounts of the new park, which opened on 19 May 1923, contradict themselves so sharply that it is difficult to know what was imagined and what was actually there, but the reports all suggest that Sarabee's new level had a deliberately provocative air, as if he had set out to construct a sinister amusement park, an inverted park of dark pleasures. We know that visitors were given a choice: either to pass through the other parks or to descend directly in any of the thirty-six elevators that had been installed on the outside of the great upper wall. Those who chose the new elevators found themselves in large, lantern-lit elevator cars operated by masked attendants costumed like devils. We do not know exactly where the Costume Pavilions were located, although it appears that visitors were urged to assume a disguise before passing through red-curtained archways into an almost dark world. The park was lit only by red and ochre lights that dimly illuminated the midnight towers, the looming buildings and black alleys, where whispers of barkers in dark doorways and bursts of honky-tonk music were punctuated with darker noises – howls, harsh voices, clashes of glass. It was a world both alluring and disturbing, a dark underworld of uncertain pleasures that made people hesitate on the threshold before deciding to lose themselves in the dark.

However exaggerated some of the accounts may be, or confused by the presence of actors and stunt men, it is clear that the park was intended to startle and shock. Many visitors simply left in anger and disgust. But large numbers remained to stroll about uneasily, peering into archways, lingering in the dark alleys, looking about as if fearful of being caught, while still others abandoned themselves utterly to the extreme and dubious pleasures of the park. Such abandonment, such release from the constraints of the upper parks, is precisely what the park seems actively to have encouraged – hence the importance of the Costume Pavilions, which, apart from adding colour and humour, served the more serious purpose of encouraging people to assume new identities. The park appears to have deliberately offered itself as a series of temptations; the crowds were continually invited to step over the very line carefully drawn in Sarabee's other parks. The complaints of scandalized visitors resulted in two separate police investigations, each of which turned up nothing, although critics of the investigation pointed out that Sarabee was more than capable of disguising the true nature of his amusements and that in any case the head of the investigations was a former roller-coaster operator in the upper park – a charge that was never substantiated.

In the face of questionable and conflicting evidence it is difficult to know how to assess the many eyewitness reports, which include disturbing accounts of a House of Horrors so frightening that visitors are reduced to fits of hysterical weeping, of fun-house mirrors that show back naked bodies in obscene postures. We hear of smoky sideshows in which the knife thrower pierces the wrists of the spangled woman on the turning wheel and the sword-swallower draws from his throat a sword red with blood. We hear of rides so violent that people are rendered unconscious or insane, of a House of Eros filled with cries of terror and ecstasy. There are reports of troubling erotic displays in a Palace of Pleasure, where female visitors fitted with special harnesses are said to drop through trapdoors into transparent pillars of glass sixty feet high, which stand in a great hall filled with masked men and women who shout and cheer at the swift but harness-controlled falls that send skirts and dresses swirling high above the hips – an erotic display that is said to take on an eerie beauty as twenty or thirty women fall screaming in the great hall lit by red, blue and green electric lights. We hear of a Lovers' Leap in which unhappy lovers chain their wrists together and jump to their deaths before crowds standing behind velvet ropes, of a Suicide Coaster built to leave the track at its highest curve and plunge to destruction in a dark field. There is talk of a Palace of Statues divided into a labyrinth of small rooms, in which replicas of famous classical statues are said to satisfy unspeakable desires. We hear of disturbing prodigies of scale-model art, such as an Oriental palace the size of a child's building block, filled with hundreds upon hundreds of chambers, corridors, stairways, dungeons and curtained recesses, and containing over five thousand figures visible only with the aid of a magnifying lens, who exhibit over three thousand varieties of sexual appetite, and there are reports of a masterful miniature of Paradise Park itself, carved out of beechwood and revealing every level in rigorous detail, from the festive upper bridges with their rides, brass bands and exotic villages to the most secret rooms of the darkest pleasure palaces in the blackest depths of the lowest level, containing over thirty thousand figures in sharply caught attitudes, the whole concealed under a silver thimble. Even taking exaggeration into account, what are we to make of a Children's Castle in which girls ten and eleven years old are said to prowl the corridors costumed as Turkish concubines, Parisian streetwalkers and famous courtesans and lure small boys and girls into hidden rooms? What are we to think of deep pleasure-pits into which visitors are encouraged to leap by howling, writhing devils, or of a Tunnel of Ecstasy, a House of Blood, a Voyage of Unearthly Delights? From these and similar reports, however unreliable, it seems clear that the new park invited violations of an extreme kind and carried certain themes to a dark fulfilment. But the park seems never to have been intrinsically unsafe; rather, the dangers lay in the rides and pleasure palaces themselves, and not in the promenades and alleys, where the costumed crowds were never violent and where serious troublemakers were led away by masked guards and dropped into straw-filled dungeons.

One of the more disturbing features of the new level, which quickly became known as Devil's Park, was the public suicides, which many visitors claimed to have witnessed, although among the witnesses were those who said it was all a hoax performed by specially trained actors. Even the majority who believed the suicides to be real were divided among themselves, some expressing moral outrage and others asserting what they called a right to suicide. The issue was brought to a head by the spectacular death of sixteen-year-old Anna Stanski, a high-school student from Brooklyn who disguised herself as a man in a porkpie hat, pushed her way through the turnstile at the top of the new Lovers' Leap, tore off her hat and set fire to her hair, and leaped flaming from the ledge before anyone could stop her – this at the very moment when a woman in her twenties and a man with wavy grey hair were having their wrists chained together by an attendant. Anna Stanski's fiery death was witnessed by hundreds of visitors, many of whom saw her lying in a field with twisted arms and a broken neck, and it was reported the next day in major newspapers across the country. The park management, forced to defend itself, argued that Anna Stanski was a troubled young woman with a history of depressive insanity, that those who accused the park of promoting public suicides were now in the odd position of having to admit that Anna Stanski's suicide actually saved two lives, since it discouraged the chained lovers from pursuing their leap, and that the park was no more responsible for her death than the City of New York was responsible for the deaths of those who leaped almost daily from its bridges and skyscrapers. Critics were quick to point out that there was a sharp distinction to be

made between the City of New York and an immoral 'amusement' that actively encouraged suicide, while others, scornful of
the claim that lives had been saved, questioned whether the
two so-called lovers were not rather actors hired to stir the
passions of the crowd. Their scorn was turned against them by
the park's defenders, who argued that if in fact the lovers were
actors, then the park could not be accused of encouraging
suicide; and they argued further that, in comparison with the
number of accidental deaths that occur in all amusement parks
and are accepted in good faith as part of the risk, the number of
suicides in Sarabee's park, whether staged or real, was trivial and
negligible, despite the grotesque attention paid to them by
antagonists whose real enemy was not suicide at all but freedom
pure and simple. The episode was soon overshadowed by a
hotel fire in Brighton, in which fourteen people died, and the
murder of minor racketeer Giambattista Salerno in a Surf
Avenue seafood restaurant.

Responses to the new park were sharply divided, but even
outraged critics who considered the park a moral disgrace
admitted that Sarabee, while forfeiting the respect he had
earned with his earlier parks, was a shrewd showman who knew
how to appeal to the debased tastes of the urban masses. Several
commentators made an effort to connect the park with the new
post-war freedom, the collapse of middle-class morality, the
indiscriminate rush towards pleasure – in short, the collective
frenzy of which Devil's Park was but the latest symptom. In an
attempt to assess the park and place it in Sarabee's career, one
critic argued that it was the embittered showman's cynical
response to his failed park: thoroughly disillusioned by failure,
Sarabee had created an anti-park, a deliberately crude and
savage park pandering to the most despicable instincts of the
crowd. This interpretation, which attracted a good deal of
attention, was answered incisively in a long article by Warren
Burchard, who after an eleven-year silence on the subject of

amusement parks returned to the charge and argued that Devil's Park, far from being an exception in Sarabee's career, was the latest expression of an unbroken line of development. Each park, the argument ran, carried the idea of the amusement park to a greater extreme. This remained true even of the failed park, which, despite its rejection of the mechanical ride, moved in the direction of newer and more intense pleasures. The history of Sarabee's parks, Burchard argued, was nothing less than an uninterrupted movement in a single direction, of which Devil's Park was not simply the latest but also the final development. For here Sarabee had dared to incorporate into his park an element that threatened the very existence of that curious institution of mass pleasure known as the amusement park: namely, an absence of limits. After this there could be no further parks, but only acts of refinement and elaboration, since any imaginable step forward could result only in the complete elimination of the idea of an amusement park. Burchard's argument was taken up and modified by a number of other critics, but it remained the classic defence of Devil's Park, against which opponents of Sarabee were forced to shape their counter-arguments.

The moral outrage directed against the new park, the conflicting reports, the rumours and exaggerations, the death of Anna Stanski, all served to pique the public's curiosity and increase attendance, despite the many people who declared they would never return; and such evidence as we have suggests that many of Sarabee's most outspoken opponents did in fact return, again and again, lured by forbidden pleasures, by the protection of masks and disguises, by the sheer need to know.

Even as controversy raged, and investigation threatened, and attendance rose, rumour had it that Sarabee was planning still another park. It was said that Sarabee was working on a ride so extraordinary that to go on it would be to change your life forever. It was said that Sarabee was developing a magical or mystical park from which the unwary visitor would never return. It was said that Sarabee was creating a park consisting of small, separate booths in which, by means of a special machine attached to the head, each immobile visitor would experience the entire range of human sensation. It was said that Sarabee was creating an invisible park, an infinite park, a park on the head of a pin. The intense and often irresponsible speculation of that winter was a clear sign that Sarabee had touched a nerve; and as the new season drew near and the last mounds of snow melted in the shadows of the bathhouses, small weekend crowds began to arrive in order to walk around the famous white wall, to stare at the great gates, the high towers, the covered elevator booths, to hover about the closed park in the hope of piercing its newest secret.

The opening was set for Saturday, 31 May 1924, at 9 a.m.; as early as Friday evening a line began to form. By 6.30 the following morning the crowd was so dense that mounted police were called in to keep order. The eyewitness reports differ in important details, but most agree that shouts were heard from inside the park at about seven o'clock. A few minutes later the gates opened to let out a stream of workmen, concessionaires, actors, spielers, Mbuti tribesmen, ride operators, dwarfs and maroon-jacketed guards, all of whom were gesticulating and shouting. The first alarm was sounded shortly thereafter and witnesses recalled seeing a thin trail of smoke at the top of the wall. Within twenty minutes the entire park was in flames. The great white wall, a highly flammable structure of lath and staff that had cost a small fortune to insure, quickly became a vast ring of fire; policemen cleared the streets as chunks of flaming wall fell like meteors and threw up showers of sparks. By the third alarm, fire engines were arriving from every firehouse in Brooklyn. As part of the wall collapsed, spectators could see the flaming rides within: the merry-go-round with its fiery roof and its circle of burning horses, the hellish Ferris wheel turning in a sheet of fire, the collapsing bridges, the blackened roller-coaster with its blazing wooden struts, the fiery booths and falling towers. Suddenly a cry went up: from one of the rotundas leading to the first underground park there rose a flock of flaming seagulls, crying a high, pained cry. Some of them flew in crazed circles directly into the crowd, where people screamed and covered their faces and beat the air with their hands.

By nine in the morning firemen were fighting only to contain the raging fire and save neighbouring property; hoses poured water on the blistering façades of side-street boarding-houses and a police launch was sent to rescue nine fishermen trapped at the end of a blazing pier. Suddenly a sideshow lion, its mane on fire, leaped over a flaming section of wall and ran screaming in pain into the street. Three policemen with drawn revolvers chased it into a parking lot, where it sprang onto the hood of a parked car. They shot it twenty times in the head and then smashed its skull with an axe. By ten o'clock a portion of ground caved in and fell to the park below, which was also in flames; spectators from the tops of nearby buildings could see down into a pit of fire, which was consuming the two hotels, the six bathhouses, the shops, the restaurants, the underground roller-coaster and House of Mirth. The fiery lower pier fell hissing into the artificial ocean, throwing up dark clouds of acrid smoke; and from the flames there rose again a flock of crazed and shrieking gulls, their backs and wings on fire, turning and spinning through the smoke and flames, until at last, one by one, they plunged down like stones.

By noon the fire was under control, although it continued to rage on every level all afternoon and far into the night. By the following morning Paradise Park was a smoking field of rubble and wet ashes. Here and there rose a few blackened and stunted structures: the melted metal housing of a Ferris-wheel motor, the broken concrete pediment of some vanished ride, clumps of curled iron. Somehow – the papers called it a miracle – only a single human life was lost, although innumerable lions, tigers, monkeys, pumas, elephants and camels perished in the fire, as well as the seagulls of the first underground level. The single body, discovered in the debris of the deepest level and damaged beyond recognition, was assumed by many to be Sarabee himself, an assumption that seemed confirmed by the disappearance of the showman and the discovery, in his Surf Avenue office, of a signed letter transferring ownership of the park to Danziker in the event of Sarabee's death. Some, it is true, insisted that the evidence was by no means conclusive and that Sarabee had simply slipped away in another disguise. Although the cause of the fire was never determined, a strong suspicion of arson was never put to rest; reports from inside the park suggested that the fire had not spread from one level to another but had broken out on all levels simultaneously. The papers vied with one another in proclaiming it Sarabee's Greatest Show, or Another Sarabee Spectacular; the crude headlines may have contained a secret truth. For as Warren Burchard expressed it in a memorable obituary article, the fiery destruction of Paradise Park was the 'logical last step' in a series of increasingly violent pleasures: after the extreme inventions of Devil's Park, only the dubious thrill of total destruction remained. Sarabee, the article continued, recognizing the inevitability of the next step, had designed the fire and arranged his own death, since to survive the completed circle of his parks was unthinkable. The historian can only note that such arguments, however attractive, however irrefutable, are not subject to the laws of evidence; and that we know as fact only that Paradise Park was utterly destroyed in a conflagration that lasted some twenty-six hours and caused an estimated eight million dollars in property damage.

It is nevertheless true that the brief history of Paradise Park, when separated from legend, may lead even the most cautious historian to wonder whether certain kinds of pleasure, by their very nature, do not seek more and more extreme forms until, utterly exhausted but unable to rest, they culminate in the black ecstasy of annihilation.

The ruined park was repossessed by the City of New York, which filled in the underground levels and turned the upper level into an extension of the parking lot that covered the remainder of the old Dreamland property; the enlarged parking lot became a public park in 1934 under the administration of Fiorello La Guardia and has remained a park to this day. Here and there in shady corners of the park, on hot summer afternoons, it is said that you can feel the earth move slightly and hear, far below, the faint sound of subterranean merry-go-rounds and the cries of perishing animals.

In 1926 a paper presented by Coney Island historian John Carter Dixon to the Brooklyn Historical Society revealed that no one called Warren Burchard had ever worked for the *Brooklyn Eagle*. Later evidence uncovered by Dixon showed that the name had been invented by Sarabee as part of a promotional campaign. Although the author of the Burchard articles is unknown, Dixon suggests that they were written by one of Sarabee's press agents and touched up by Sarabee himself, who appears to have had a hand in his own obituary notice.

Seventy years after the destruction of Paradise Park, Sarabee's legacy remains an ambiguous one. His most daring innovations have been ignored by later amusement-park entrepreneurs, who have been content to move in the direction of the safe, wholesome, family park. Sarabee, himself the inventor of a classic park, was driven by some dark necessity to push beyond all reasonable limits to more dangerous and disturbing inventions. He comes at the end of the era of the first great American amusement parks, which he carried to technological and imaginative limits unsurpassed in his time, and he set an example of restless invention that has remained unmatched in the history of popular pleasure.

A book of photographs called *Old New York*, published by Arc

Books in 1957 and long out of print, contains fourteen views of Paradise Park: nine pictures of the upper level, including two of Paradise Alley, and five of the first underground level. The one most evocative of a vanished era shows a group of male bathers in sleeveless dark bathing costumes standing with their hands on their hips in the artificial surf before the criss-cross iron braces of the underground pier, with its gabled wooden roof, its arches and turrets, its flying flags. Some of the men stare boldly and even sternly at the camera, while others, with powerful shoulders and thick moustaches, are smiling in an easy, boyish-manly, innocent way that seems at one with the knee-high water, the pier, the ocean air, the unseen festive park.

Kaspar Hauser speaks

Ladies and gentlemen of Nuremberg. Distinguished guests. It is with no small measure of amazement that I stand before you today, on the occasion of the third anniversary of my arrival in your city. When I recall the brutish creature, half idiot and half animal, who appeared suddenly in your streets that day – a creature jabbering unintelligibly – stumbling – weeping – blinded by daylight – a hunched and stunted creature – lost – unutterably lost – a creature who from his earliest years had been shut up in a dark dungeon – and when I next consider the frock-coated and impeccably cravated young gentleman you see before your eyes – then, I confess, I am seized by a kind of spiritual dizziness. It's as if I were nothing but a dream, a fantastic dream – your dream, ladies and gentlemen of Nuremberg. For whatever I may be, I who was buried deeper than the dead, I am always mindful how very much I am your creation. Through the patient guidance of Professor Daumer, to whom my gratitude is boundless, I have been formed in your image. I am you – and you – and you – I who only a few short years ago was lower than any beast.

I understand of course that my progress is far from complete. About this matter I have no illusions. When I enter a room I am fully aware of the stray looks of amusement or pity, to say nothing of those subtler and more harmful looks that may be described as the polite suppression of amusement or pity. Even now, as a full-grown man of twenty, I cannot hold my arms in a natural way, but can feel them hanging awkwardly at my sides, the fingers slightly outspread. My manner of walking is uncertain. This is especially so when I feel myself the centre of attention: then I advance in a kind of delicate lurch, or as if I were falling forward and then quickly moving my feet in order to remain upright. Nor am I absolute master of my face, which now and then will break into a scowl, or reveal a look of childlike astonishment. Even my words don't always emerge with the fluency I long for, but come forth in rushed clusters, or with unnatural slowness. Sometimes I stumble into a pit or well of sadness, a deep pit, a long fall; the sheer walls soar; and as I fall, never reaching the bottom, for there is no bottom, I stare up and see, far above, in the little circle of light that is always receding, faces peering down at me, faces unimaginably high up – and they are your faces, ladies and gentlemen of Nuremberg. For though I have been formed in your image, yet at the same time I am so far beneath you that the effort of looking up at you makes me giddy. That much is clear.

Nevertheless, despite these flaws in my progress, I think I may say that I have come a remarkably long way. Certainly it is remarkable that I am able to stand upright before you today, after a lifetime of being shackled to the ground. But I needn't rehearse for you my well-known history. Let two examples suffice. I remember an incident that took place shortly after my arrival here, during the time when I was kept in the Vestner Tower of the castle. One day my prison-keeper, who always treated me gently, carried in to me an object I had never seen before. It was a kind of stick, which I could scarcely see, because in my ignorance of the world I could not yet distinguish objects clearly; but there was something bright and shining at the top, which pleased me and attracted my deepest interest. My keeper set it down on a table. With a feeling of excitement and delight I reached out my hand. The stick bit me. I gave a startled cry and snatched my hand away. I could see a look of alarm on my keeper's face, an alarm that disturbed me even more than the dangerous stick. What had I done wrong? Why had the stick hurt me? Ah, the stick, the stick, ladies and gentlemen – you know the stick, do you? But as for me, I knew nothing except terror and pain.

I pass on to the second incident. I was visited in the tower one day by a gentleman stranger, not long before I was moved to Professor Daumer's home. Herr von Feuerbach had a kind but searching look, and after a number of questions he led me to the place in the wall of the tower where, from a safe distance, I liked to look up at the brightness. He seemed aware of the tenderness of my eyes and was careful to position me at one side of the dangerous place. With words and gestures he indicated that I should look down at what lay before me. I obeyed. Immediately I was overcome by anxiety and a terrible sense of oppression, and turning away I cried 'Ugly! Ugly!' – a word I had recently been taught. My sensation was that a window-shutter had been placed directly before me, and that on this shutter were ugly splotches of wall-paint – green and yellow and white and blue and red. At that time, you see, I had no knowledge of the changes wrought in objects by distance, indeed I had no sense of distant things; but rather, what I saw appeared as if directly before my gaze, a window-shutter splashed with ugly wall-paint, closing me in.

The stick and the shutter, ladies and gentlemen! Do you begin to understand? I was a youth of sixteen or seventeen, with a beard beginning to grow on my cheeks, and yet I had no knowledge of a candle, no faintest notion of a landscape seen from a window. I had a handful of words that had been taught to me in the tower and that I used in my own way, often to the confusion or hilarity of visitors. Shall we speak of the hilarity of visitors? No, I think not. And of course I had my little toy horses, which I liked to decorate with ribbons and pieces of coloured paper. Bright, shiny objects pleased me. I spoke to my horses, I spoke to my bread. I was a child – no, I was less than a child, I was scarcely more than a toad. One day I was taken for a walk in the streets, in the company of two policemen. Suddenly a black thing came towards me, a shaking black thing. Terror seized me, I tried to run away. Only later, much later, could I be made to understand that I had seen a black hen.

For even then, you see, in the castle tower, high above the roofs of the town, I was barely human. And yet, when you consider the black emptiness that was my earlier life, my earlier death, the tower was civilization itself. But can you consider it, that other life? Can you? Is it possible for you, ladies and gentlemen of Nuremberg, by the deepest, the sincerest, the most sustained effort of imagination, to understand what it means to have the sensations of a worm? To inhabit a dark place for seventeen years; seeing no light; never a face; not a voice; without even being able to feel the loss of such things – is it possible? I lived in the dark. Something prevented me from standing. I could sit up and slide a little. And perhaps, in this single instance, I may claim an advantage over you, a dubious and inglorious superiority, for I think I may say that I alone among you have experienced such an existence. Seventeen years! No, it is too difficult. Even I can scarcely imagine it. The man who looked after me never showed himself. He left the bread and water when I fell asleep. I woke always in the same dark. The ground was covered with straw. Of course the idea of cruelty didn't occur to me then. I had my water and my bread and my two little horses. They were white and made of wood. I sat with my legs straight out. I was content, or if not content, then not discontent. What did I know of such things? It was only later, when I emerged from my dungeon, that I learned the meaning of discontent. And that is something I think you should take into account, ladies and gentlemen of Nuremberg, when you contemplate my remarkable progress. For it was only in leaving myself behind that I saw what I had been, although it is equally true that by the time I was able to see myself at all, I had already advanced so far that when I glanced back I was scarcely visible.

Please understand that if I mention such things, it isn't in order to evoke your sympathy, least of all your pity, but only to remind you how confusing my new life was bound to be. For many days I couldn't endure the light. It scalded my eyes like boiling water flung in my face. Light, ladies and gentlemen! Symbol of knowledge! By this alone you can see how thoroughly my other life had indisposed me for progress.

And yet I did progress. I did. First the dungeon: then the tower. Even the tower – especially the tower – was progress of a startling kind. Was it in recognition of my unsolved nature that I was still forbidden to live on the level ground? In any case, once removed from the tower, where I was visited daily by crowds of the curious, once settled in the peace and order of Professor Daumer's family, I surged ahead. Within three months I had learned to speak, to write, to understand the difference between things that are alive, like cats, and things that only appear to be alive, like paper blown by the wind. The ball didn't roll along by itself whenever it wanted to: this too I learned, with difficulty. Who had cut the leaves into their shapes? Why did the horse on the wall not run away? Professor Daumer was very patient. I felt bursts of power and curiosity, followed always by a fall into melancholy, as I became more deeply aware of the big hole in my life. Then I would surge ahead again. One night – I remember it clearly – I saw the stars for the first time. Then did I feel an uplifting, a rapture, such as I had never known; though the plunge into despair that soon followed was deeper than that height.

My progress, as I say, was rapid, though I soon became aware that my life in the dark had sharpened my nervous system in peculiar ways. The keenness of my sight astonished Professor Daumer. I saw perfectly in the dark. In a darkened room where guests were unable to see each other at five paces, I was able to read easily from a printed book. At twilight, at a distance of one hundred paces, I was able to distinguish the single berries in a cluster of elderberries; at sixty paces I could distinguish an elderberry from a blackcurrant. My sense of smell was so sharp that for many months I suffered fits of nausea when I walked in the countryside. Flowers sickened me with their harsh perfumes. Revolting odours of drying tobacco rose from distant fields. I was able to distinguish apple, pear and plum trees from each other by the violent smell of their leaves. Indeed all odours were offensive to me except that of bread, fennel, anise and caraway – smells I had known in my dungeon. Even my sense of touch was disturbingly keen. The touch of a hand affected me like a blow.

How well I remember my first sight of the full moon. It was from a window in Professor Daumer's house, in summer. The room was warm, summer-night warm, but my body felt suddenly cold. I began to shiver. I felt a pressure on my chest. I kept looking at the moon, the big white moon, the big big bigger and bigger moon, which seemed too big for the sky, too big for the entire world. My eyes burned, I was shivering, shivering. When I looked away, everything was white.

Yes, my nerves were sharp in those days – so sharp that I could feel the presence of hidden metals in a room, by a tugging sensation in my body. Professor Daumer performed experiments, which he carefully wrote down. Visitors came and observed my unusual capacities, and spread word of them. Gradually, in the course of a year, as I grew accustomed to the strange new world into which I had burst, like a barbarian into Rome – for I have read your books, ladies and gentlemen – the unpleasant acuteness of my sensations weakened, until at present they are nearly normal, except for my ability to distinguish objects in the dark.

I will say nothing here of the bloody attempt on my life by the man in black, which took place one morning when Professor Daumer had gone for a walk and which first brought me to the attention of Europe.

Now I stand before you, a civilized man, a rational man, in certain respects a remarkable man: a Wundermensch, as I have been called. No doubt it is wonderful to have passed through twenty years of mental life in the space of a few short years. It is precisely this leap that has enabled me to become one of you, or nearly so, for as I have said, there are little flaws in the copy, little imperfections that give me away, especially to myself. Even the leap of which I speak, the tremendous leap towards you and away from me, a leap that leaves the bruise of my heels in my own sides – even this leap is no more than a sign of my difference.

And this brings me to the real subject of my address, namely, the inner life, the intimate feelings, of Kaspar Hauser. What is it like to be Kaspar? For people look at me and wonder. You too, ladies and gentlemen, you who have come to look and hear – you too have wondered: what is it like? For I think it fair to say that I am interesting to you. I am a riddle, an enigma that cannot be solved. Can it be that you are in need of riddles? For after all, you know yourselves through and through, you who are not enigmas; perhaps you are tired of yourselves; perhaps you've come to the end of yourselves; you have filled yourselves with yourselves to the very edges of your being; so that now it is time for – let us say, for Kaspar Hauser. But then, aren't you in danger of a contradiction? For if I am interesting to you precisely to the extent that I'm not one of you, then your desire to civilize me, to turn me into a good citizen of Nuremberg, can lead to nothing but loss of interest. Is it possible then that what you secretly desire is to be through with Kaspar Hauser, that irritating enigma, that grotesque mistake, whose childlike stares and melancholy smiles are alike intolerable? But I mention this only in passing. For I was about to tell you what it is like to be Kaspar Hauser. I have brooded over this question ever since I've had words to brood with, and I believe I am ready to tell you now.

To be Kaspar Hauser is to long, at every moment of your dubious existence, with every fibre of your questionable being, not to be Kaspar Hauser. It's to long to leave yourself completely behind, to vanish from your own sight. Does this surprise you? It is of course what you have taught me to desire. And I am a diligent student. With your help I have furnished myself inside and out. My thoughts are yours. These words are yours. Even my black and bitter tears are yours, for I shed them at the thought of the life I never had, which is to say, your life, ladies and gentlemen of Nuremberg. My deepest wish is not to be an exception. My deepest wish is not to be a curiosity, an object of wonder. It is to be unremarkable. To become you – to sink into you – to merge with you until you cannot tell me from yourselves; to be uninteresting; to be nothing at all; to experience the ecstasy of mediocrity – is it so much to ask? You who have helped me to advance so far, won't you lead me to the promised land, the tranquil land of the ordinary, the banal, the boring? Not to be Kaspar Hauser, not to be the enigma of Europe, not to be the wild boy in the tower, the man without a childhood, the young man without a youth, the monster born in the middle of his life, but to be you, to be you, to be nothing but you! This is my vision of paradise. And although the very existence of such a vision reveals nothing so much as my distance, which widens into an abyss even as I try to fling myself across, still I am not without hope.

For just as my nervous sensibilities have lessened, in the course of my short sojourn in the realm of light, so have other changes been wrought. The world has come to seem less and less mysterious to me. No longer do I feel a childish wonder when I look up at the night sky full of stars. My extraordinary zeal for learning, noted by Professor Daumer and many visitors, has gradually given way to a steady, reasonable diligence. My memory, which at first astonished the world, is now neither more nor less than it ought to be. When I discover that I am ignorant of something, I learn what is necessary and no more. Many have remarked upon my practical nature, my good common sense. I am told that my gaze remains childish, my smile melancholy and rueful; before the mirror I practise other expressions. My speech, though still imperfect, has become less rough, without harsh edges; above all I love common words, familiar phrases, into which I disappear as into a warm shadow. Sometimes I feel that I am slowly erasing myself, in order for someone else to appear, the one I long for, who will not resemble me. Then I think of my assassin, whose breath, on my neck, I feel in the night. Is it possible that he, the dark whisperer, will fulfil my deepest desire? For when the knife, which already is plunging towards me, sinks deep into my chest, then at last I will no longer know what it is to be Kaspar, but will leave him behind forever.

Thank you for listening to me today, and if in the course of my remarks I have said anything to offend you, please forgive poor Kaspar Hauser, who would not harm the meanest insect that crawls in dung – far less you, ladies and gentlemen of Nuremberg.

Beneath the cellars of our town

1

Beneath the cellars of our town, far down, there lies a maze of twisting and intersecting passageways, stretching away in every direction and connected to the upper surface by stairways of rough stone. The origin of the passageways remains unclear. Although there is some evidence that they were known to the Indians who preceded the first white settlers, our historians are unable to decide whether the passageways are the result of natural process or whether they represent an ancient form of subterranean architecture. Our earliest records, which go back to 1646, the year of our incorporation, make mention of a 'tunnel' or 'cave' that is said to be located 'under the ground'. The words have led some to argue that our passageways were originally a single long passage, to which later ones were added by deliberate design. Such evidence as we can gather neither refutes nor supports this hypothesis.

2

The passageways vary considerably in width, though even the broadest give an impression of narrowness because of the extreme height of the walls. The darkness is dimly relieved by old-fashioned oil lamps in the shape of glass globes, which hang from brackets projecting from the walls at irregular intervals some fifteen feet above the ground. Sometimes a path turns sharply downwards, and may in time pass beneath the structure of passageways into a lower level that is simply a twisting continuation of the one above. This level in turn may lead downwards to still lower passageways. The paths are of hard earth. Small stones or fragments of fallen rock lie about. Here and there a black puddle gleams at the base of a wall.

3

We descend through openings that lie scattered throughout the township, not only in the north woods but also in parking lots behind the stores on Main Street, in the slopes of the railroad embankment, in the picnic grounds overlooking the creek, in the Revolutionary War graveyard, in weed-grown vacant lots and backyard gardens, at the edges of school yards, at the back of the long shed in the lumber yard, behind the green dumpster at the back of the car wash, beside yellow fire hydrants and dark blue mailboxes on maple-lined streets rippling with sun and shade. No one knows how many openings actually exist, for new ones are continually being discovered, while old ones collapse or are condemned as unsafe or are covered over by forest growth or the clumsiness of backhoes and bulldozers. A few openings have been given a kind of architectural permanence: in back of the town hall the opening has been surrounded by a circular platform of polished granite, on which a circle of white wooden columns stands in support of a domed roof, and here and there, on street corners or in parking lots, you see simple structures composed of two square posts under a peaked roof covered with black or red asbestos shingles. Most of the openings, however, remain impermanent and inconspicuous. The stone stairways are steep and sometimes circular; at the bottom there is always a short path that leads through an arched opening into a winding passageway.

4

As small children we are brought down to the passageways by our parents, who hold us tightly by the hand and point at the dim-shining globed lamps, the soaring walls, the sharply turning paths. It's as if we were being introduced to the movie theatre, or the library, or the nature trails in the north woods, but we're aware of a difference, for we sense in our parents both a gravity and a quickening that we haven't sensed before. Some of us are frightened and pull away, towards the stairway and the sunlight. Others are enchanted, as if they have stepped into a picture in a storybook. Children are forbidden to wander the passageways alone and it is only in adolescence that we begin to wander freely, seeing in the dark and turning distances images of our secret rapture or despair. As we grow older we tend to spend less time in the passageways, for the cares of life pull us away, and it may happen that some of us recall the winding pathways beneath our town as one recalls some half-forgotten journey far back in the depths of childhood. Often in old age we find ourselves spending more and more hours in the cool passageways, which are believed to be healthful, though a small number of our older citizens avoid them altogether. But even those whose lives are largely passed above are never forgetful of the world below, which seems to tug at the soles of our shoes as we stroll along the clean, sun-sparkling streets.

5

Some say that we descend in order to lose our way. And yet it remains true that never once in the long history of our town has anyone failed to find the way back. For not only do our citizens descend whenever they like through widely scattered openings, but lamplighters in peaked caps move from place to place, to say nothing of the watchmen who quietly make their rounds, resting their thumbs in their broad belts, or the workers in their hard hats and green uniforms, who set up wooden sawhorses and orange safety cones as they clear fallen rocks into wheelbarrows, prop up decaying ceilings, or widen a path with sharp blows of their picks. And even if, as often happens, we wander for hours, or perhaps days, without meeting a soul in the turning dark, there's always the likelihood of a sudden arch in the wall, leading to a stairway going up. But this once granted, it must be admitted that there is never a sense, in the passageways, of knowing where you are. The pattern of twisting and interconnecting paths, on several levels, is far too complex for anyone to master, and in addition the pattern is always changing, for old passageways become suddenly or gradually impassable, and new wall-openings and small connecting corridors are continually being formed by the fall of rock fragments or the gradual loosening of rock along fault lines – a process regularly enhanced by the workers with their busy picks. One should also keep in mind the frequent burning out of the lamps, despite the vigilance of the lamplighters, and the consequent long stretches of unilluminated darkness. For all these reasons it isn't too much to say that after the first few twists and turns at the bottom of a familiar stairway we enter uncertain ground. But this is by no means the same thing as losing our way, so that if indeed we descend for that reason, then we continually fail. Perhaps it would be better, for those who hold this theory of descent, to say that we descend in order to have before us the perpetual possibility of losing our way.

6

A further objection presents itself. To say that we descend in order to lose our way, or in order to have before us the perpetual possibility of losing our way, implies that our lives above-ground are simple, orderly and calm. This is certainly not the case. Although ours is a relatively quiet town, we suffer disease, disappointment and death as all men and women do, and if we choose to descend into our passageways and wander the branching paths, who dares to say what passion draws us into our dark?

7

Flint and jasper arrowheads, stone axeheads, bone fishhooks, ear pendants of stone and shell, an earthenware pot with a circular lip curving outwards, a mortar for grinding maize, fire-blackened stones – such are the evidences of Indian life that have been discovered in the dirt paths and rock walls of our passageways, and that today are displayed in a basement room of our historical society. Experts have identified the artefacts as belonging to the Quinnepaug tribe of the Algonquian linguistic stock. We know that the Quinnepaugs had a word for the passageways, meaning either 'tunnel' or 'channel', as well as several obscure words apparently referring to particular openings or stairways. What we don't know is what use the Indians made of the passageways. Some of our historians believe that the Quinnepaugs hid from enemies in the underground dark, while others suggest that rituals of propitiation or prayer may have been conducted below. One school insists that early in their history the Quinnepaugs abandoned the upper world to dwell in the passageways, from which they emerged only to hunt at night and to bury their dead; a dubious offshoot of this school argues that pale, wraith-like descendants of the tribe still live in secret hollows of the walls, dreaming of past glory and slipping out from time to time to move silently along unfrequented paths. We ourselves, who would like nothing better than to believe in silent Indians haunting our passageways, sometimes try to imagine stern warriors and black-haired squaws moving stealthily behind us in the always branching dark, but when we turn suddenly we see only a shadowy path, a fissured wall, a tremor of blackness.

8

It often happens that citizens of other towns ridicule our passageways, or subject them to sharp attack. The lower air, they say, is unhealthy, and gives to our citizens a certain characteristic and unpleasant pallor. Noxious effluvia, rising from cracks in the ceilings of passageways, seep into our soil, penetrate the roots of vegetables in our gardens, soak into our cellars and taint the very air breathed by babies in the cradles of our homes. As if such charges weren't enough to sting us into reply, our passageways are also said to weaken the foundations of our homes and even to undermine the stability of the entire town, which at any moment is liable to collapse. Although there is no slightest evidence to support such assertions, we carefully refute every charge, conducting extensive tests, hiring outside engineers, studying soil samples, comparing shades of pallor in twenty-six towns. But no sooner have we finished defending ourselves than we find ourselves under attack again. Our passageways, we are told, are useless, or frivolous, or wasteful, or worse. For what purpose can they be said to serve except to distract us from the serious conduct of our lives and to tempt us towards a kind of childish dreaminess? These are the most dangerous attacks of all, the ones intended to crush our spirit and discredit us in our own eyes. In response to such charges we have learned, over time, the value of silence.

9

Sometimes, when we travel to other towns, we experience a sense of liberation from our passageways. The sidewalks, streets and parks of alien towns have for us a peculiar charm, a kind of sunny innocence, uninterrupted as they are by stone stairways plunging below. Citizens of these towns, who spend their lives on the surface of the earth, seem to us to have a storybook quaintness about them. But soon the flat streets and sidewalks, stretching levelly away, fill us with unease. We long for our under-paths, which perhaps we haven't entered for weeks, nor can we rest until we have fled the rigid towns and entered voluptuously our dark, yielding passageways.

10

Although we defend our passageways relentlessly against the lies and misrepresentations of outsiders, it remains true that we ourselves are not without our disagreements. One source of contention is the sheer bareness of the passageways, which strikes some of our more practical citizens as disturbing. From time to time a motion is presented before the town council requesting permission for a soft-drink or hot-dog concession in the empty spaces stretching away below, or for more imaginative enterprises – stationary pushcarts displaying kitchenware or leather boots, a sidewalk café, bookstalls, a new kind of microwave vending machine offering hot roast chicken legs and steaming bagels. The business managers and small merchants who favour such ventures are in no sense fanatics or lunatics intent on betraying the history of our passageways by vulgar acts of commerce. In fact they can and do point to historical precedents. Our records show clearly that in the early eighteenth century, young boys hired by merchants and known as hawkers were permitted to roam the passageways with sacks containing biscuits and small raisin cakes called 'snappers'. There is also evidence that towards the middle of the century small stalls were set up in certain passageways, a practice that seems to have disappeared after the Revolutionary War. But it was only in the last quarter of the nineteenth century that the passageways were suddenly freed from all constraints and opened to the full fury of merchant ambition. On both sides of the wider paths stood stalls and booths with striped awnings selling Panama hats, shirtwaists, cigars in cedar-wood boxes, hot peanuts in paper twists, ivory-headed walking sticks, majolica vases, horse blankets, ploughshares, spools of thread. Period engravings show moustached men in bowlers and tight-corseted women under broad hats heaped with fruit standing in a crush between long lanes of merchandise piled high on stands, in the glare and sharp shadows cast by lamps hanging from the booths and stalls. An atmosphere of the Oriental bazaar haunts these images. One disturbing sketch shows a horse half-rearing in a narrow passageway that seems to press on both sides as a man in a top hat tries to pull him forward and the horse-dealer stands huddled in a corner holding a fistful of ten-dollar bills. These heady days of business ended abruptly with the great fire of 1901, in which twenty-six people died; in a new law passed the following year, the land beneath our town was declared exempt from business transactions of any kind.

11

But why, we are asked, should commerce be banished from our passageways? What sense does it make? It isn't a matter of developers harming a lush environment, or destroying valuable wildlife; the only life ever seen below is a thin growth of moss in the artificial light of our oil lamps. Surely a discreet form of commerce, it is suggested, such as an occasional stylish manne-quin modelling a dark blue suit or tan trench coat, would not be out of place. Against all such proposals we argue that commerce introduces a distraction into our quiet passageways; that it goes against the spirit of our under-town, which invites solitary and meditative wandering; that in any case it's unnecessary for merchants to seek space underground, since we continue to invite new businesses into our upper-town and energetically encourage business growth in every way. All such arguments are nothing but variations of a single argument that is never made but always understood: the lower world must at all costs be kept distinct from the upper. The selling of goods is an invasion of the lower world by the upper, an expansion of the town downwards. By banishing commerce we assert the absolute separateness of the lower realm, its radical difference, even if we can't agree, even if we scarcely understand, why that difference matters.

12

Repeated measurements of our passageways have led to conflicting results, in part because very few of the paths end in a clear and decisive way. Some say that all passageways once came to an end at the precise boundaries of our town. Others argue that the passageways, though limited in space, are in effect endless, winding in and out of each other in an intricate design that represents the boundless; a minor and much-ridiculed school claim that the paths wind beneath towns and hills and ocean floors in a great underworld circle of passageways. We who have wandered beneath our town from earliest childhood know that many paths grow narrower and narrower until, without ending, they become impassable. In the shadowy half-dark we peer into the narrow crevices, which vanish in blackness.

13

Now and then it comes about that our passageways are closed for repairs. Blue velvet ropes are stretched across the tops of stairways, or across the lower arches that open onto the passageways. Even though we know that the repairs will last for only a few days, a restlessness comes over us. In the hot summer days we find ourselves retreating to our cool cellars, where we sweep up flakes of plaster that have fallen from the walls, examine the water pipes for signs of rust or leakage, assemble piles of things to be thrown away: old coils of garden hose grown stiff as pipes, dusty damp gift catalogues. Sometimes at night, when we wake and cannot fall back to sleep, we go down to our cellars and walk about in the dark, smelling the familiar damp. In the stillness of the night we hear or imagine we hear a scratching or scraping: the secret digging of tunnels, in the cellars of our town.

14

At times we experience a violent craving for heights, we tunnel wanderers, we under-creepers and travellers in the dark. Then we climb into our attics or onto our sloping roofs, ascend to the belfry of our tallest church and look out past the great iron bell at our streets and rooftops, ride to the top of Indian Hill with a picnic lunch, gaze up with envy at workers at the tops of telephone poles or at the top of the high water tank with its S-shaped stairway. In the sunny offices of travel agencies we find ourselves lingering over glossy brochures showing high white hotels, white-capped blue mountains, wondrous skyscrapers that seem to reach all the way to the sun. We brood over the virtues of sunlight and the upper view, reproach ourselves for our underground lives, our blind burrowing in the dark. But the time comes when the heights displease us; the brightness hurts our eyes and prevents us from seeing; the blue skies beat against our skulls like hammerblows. Puzzled by the failure of the high view, we return with relief to our dark and branching passageways. Sometimes it seems to us that only there, under the ground, do we experience the true exhilaration of height: the town itself, imagined from below.

15

It's possible, for those who know nothing about our passageways, to imagine them as monotonous, empty and devoid of surprise. In a superficial sense this is certainly true. The dirt paths are only dirt paths; no decorations or furnishings divert the eye. From behind the next bend, no startling sight (a crystal cave, a minotaur) shocks us into wonder. One might argue that the aisles of a supermarket, bursting with colour, are far more exciting than our dull world below. But for those of us who know our passageways, the very thought of monotony is preposterous. For one thing, the passageways are continually widening and narrowing, so that you experience distinct and always changing sections. For another, the rocky walls are rough and irregular, marked by fissures, recesses, ledges, cracks, bulges, nooks and cave-like openings; and the paths, though smooth in a general way, are pitted here and there, littered with small stones and spotted with dampness or small puddles. In addition, our passageways are repeatedly intersected by other passageways, which lead off in other directions, so that very quickly you lose a sense of familiarity and feel that you've embarked on a new journey; and new passageways are always being discovered by workers as they repair older passageways, which themselves are continually changing as a result of natural forces and the picks of workers. And when you keep in mind that these always changing paths don't move on a single level, but from time to time dip downwards and pass under other passageways; and when you also keep in mind that this vertical system of passageways is so tangled and complex that there is no agreement on the number of levels, some maintaining that there are three distinct levels, others four, or five, or two, and still others – a minority, to be sure – insisting that under the lowest level there is always another level, awaiting discovery; then it ought to be clear why we never experience monotony in our passageways, but on the contrary a sensation of pleasurable uncertainty, of surprise and adventure. When all is said and done, what we feel, when we go down among our passageways, is a sensation of expansion – as if some inner constriction were suddenly bursting.

16

Some years ago a town meeting was held to consider this proposal: that we leave our homes and move permanently into the passageways. Arguments of all kinds were advanced by the advocates of the proposal, who claimed that our repeated descents were proof of our deepest desires. It was even said by some that the town itself served no purpose other than to make descent possible. Such intemperate arguments were easy to ridicule but difficult to refute, for all of us feel the deep attraction of the passageways and can, at a pinch, imagine a world without our town, but not without our passageways. The strongest counter-argument was therefore not a defence of the town, or praise of the virtues of life in the upper world, or a meticulous explanation of the impracticability of living below the ground, but rather this: our absolute certainty that, should we actually leave the upper world and move into our passageways, not a week would pass before, in the blackness beneath the dark paths, we began digging new, deeper passageways.

17

Sometimes, rounding the bend of a passageway, you come upon a lamplighter. The event is so rare that it's accounted a piece of good luck, like seeing a praying mantis on a weedstalk in a field. In their dark green uniforms and peaked caps the lamplighters look very much alike, an effect exaggerated by their silence – they nod, but never speak – and by the fact that they are all slow-moving elderly men, of approximately the same size. The tradition of the lamplighter is as old as our town, though their duties have changed: the earliest lamplighters placed flaming torches (pinewood dipped in tar) in iron supports driven into the rock walls. Not until the first years of the nineteenth century do oil lamps begin to replace the crude but striking torches, which were said to cast dramatic shadows as the torches crackled and the flames rose and fell high in the dark. Our modern lamplighters carry long aluminium poles with two separate attachments at the top: a small metal box that emits a flame for lighting extinguished wicks and a larger container, shaped like a bowl and provided with a spout, containing kerosene. Sometimes, perhaps once in a lifetime, like a vision in the dark, you see a lamplighter at the top of a tall and very narrow ladder, adjusting or replacing a lamp. Proposals for a system of underground wiring and electric light have been made since the early years of the twentieth century, but they are regularly voted down. Our enemies accuse us of a debilitating nostalgia, a refusal to enter the modern world, but we know that the real reason, the secret reason, is that we would not willingly do without our dreamlike lamplighters, whose slow and silent movements beneath our town soothe us like tides.

18

Nostalgia! No, that is a charge that irritates us profoundly, one that we take particular pains to refute. If nostalgia is the craving for a past way of life no longer possible, then we ask our accusers: what vanished way of life can possibly be represented by our bare, winding passageways? With pride we point to our town's modern features – our satellite dishes and solar panels, our new barium-sulphur street lights, our highway department's up-to-the-minute graders, pavers and rollers, our new waste-disposal plant. We are a late-twentieth-century town poised for the plunge into the new millennium, and if we honour our Revolutionary War dead and preserve our restored town hall on its original seventeenth-century green, if we dutifully place shiny bronze plaques on our eighteenth-century houses and display Quinnepaug axeheads in the basement of our historical society, we are in no sense looking back misty-eyed towards some vanished way of life that none of us could tolerate, but are merely holding on to a few keepsakes and old family photo-graphs as we make our difficult way through life like everyone else. Our passageways have nothing to do with some earlier, simpler way of life; though we can't say, don't know, what our passageways are, it would be far truer to say that they bear no relation whatever to any period of our history, but rather exist as a place apart – a place from which to contemplate the town coolly, or even to forget the town altogether.

19

One school of philosophy has suggested that all towns are like our town, but that only we believe in our passageways. It is our belief that permits us to descend, just as it is their incredulity that condemns them to the surface of earth. A corollary of this theory, proposed by a rival school, is that our passageways do not exist except insofar as we believe in them – that the entire structure of stairways, shadows and turning paths lies solely within us. Members of this school insist that the only way to find an opening to our underground world is to seek out a quiet and secluded spot. Close your eyes. Concentrate your attention inward. Descend.

20

For the rest of us, the stairways are most certainly there. We have only to walk along the railway embankment at the back of the stores on Main Street, or step behind the peeling red shed in the lumber yard, or wander in the north woods, where sooner or later we're bound to come upon a fallen and decaying tree that partly conceals a rough opening with stairs going down. Carefully we descend the rough stone steps, from which blades of grass stick up, and on which, as we make our way down, patches of moss begin to appear. At the bottom we walk a short distance to a crude archway, over which a glass-globed lamp dimly glows, and stepping through the arch we come to a passageway, stretching right and left into the dark. Sometimes we wander only to the next archway before climbing back to the everyday world. Sometimes we wander for hours, or for an entire day. But however long we wander, however deep we plunge, the time always comes when we return. Indeed it is somewhat misleading to think of us as always leaving our town to descend into our passageways. It would be no less fair to think of us as continually emerging from our passageways, into the upper town. For surely the truth of our way of life lies here, in the continual act of descent and ascent. This up-and-down movement is so striking in our lives that one school of thought has chosen the stairway rather than the passageway as our secret symbol. Even we who have no interest in symbols, we citizens who refuse to bind ourselves to any school, readily acknowledge that we are people of the stairway – uppers-and-downers, we, through and through. Those who dislike us say that we are restless, dissatisfied souls, forever escaping one place for another; though we defend ourselves sharply, we know that we can't entirely evade this charge. Those more kindly disposed prefer to think of us as continually immersing ourselves in two necessary atmospheres. For if I have spoken of the exhilaration of descent, it is necessary to speak also of a second exhilaration, the exhilaration of return: the sun striking the sidewalk, the trembling blue air, the breeze heavy with town-smells: smell of porches and warm baseball gloves on sunny summer afternoons, of cut grass and creosoted telephone poles, tang of lawnmower gasoline in the tar-scented air. And over there, that shimmering red roof, that shout, that face vivid as fire. For when we emerge, we cellar seekers, then for an instant the lost world enters us like a sword, before settling to rest. Then we seem to understand something that we had forgotten, before confusion returns. You who mock us, you laughers and surface-crawlers, you restless sideways-sliders and flatland voyagers – don't we irk you, don't we exasperate you, we mole-folk, we pale amphibians?